Temptations
Tests
And
Snares

Overcoming Obstacles
On the Way
To Your Destiny

Rev. Phyllis J. Rawlins

PRESS

Xulon Press
10640 Main Street
Suite 204
Fairfax, VA 22030
(703) 934-4411
XulonPress.com

To ord

Destiny Seekers International, Inc.

Rev. Phyllis J. Rawlins
President and Founder

PM6 149
3330 Cobb Parkway, Suite 17
Acworth, GA 30101

1-866-777-8393
Cell 770-378-5915
Fax 770-974-6583
www.destinyseekersinternational.com

In Loving Memory

Of my twin brother, Phillip Baker, who recently passed from time into eternity, and from the "Fires of Affliction" to a "glorious inheritance with all the saints in light".

The legacy of his winsome ways, his childlike faith, and his remarkable devotion to duty, lives on.

* * * * * * * * * * * * * *

With Love

To my sister, Helen Symons Alm, who never stopped believing in me, and whose encouragement and love has given me the courage to "ride out the storms" in my own life.

God Bless You, Helen.

* * * * * * * * * * * * * *

Acknowledgments

With Deep Gratitude

To my wonderful friend, Rev. Reed Maxwell, who has been to me, the embodiment of God's unconditional love.

Thank you.

* * * * * * * * * * * * * *

With Special Thanks

To my son, Jeffery D. Rawlins, who has been, along with his brothers, Jeremy and Joshua, more of a blessing than words can describe, and who has been instrumental in helping me walk out the destiny that God has for me.

* * * * * * * * * * * * * *

To Kathy Boyer – a wonderful friend that "sticketh closer than a brother", and without whose love, support, and practical assistance this book would have never been completed.

Contents

Introduction

As Christians who are born "from above" and empowered by His Spirit, our covenant privilege is to walk in victory over all of the "temptations, tests, and snares" of the enemy.

Jesus commanded us to "Be of good cheer, for I have overcome the world". (John 16:33b RSV). Inherent in this victory statement is the promise that because He overcame, we too, can overcome the powers of darkness, as we walk out our destinies in this world.

Why, then are so many Christians living defeated lives?

Why does the enemy of our souls appear to have the upper hand in our marriages, families, churches, and in situations of personal hardship and temptation?

Scripture says that satan will actually step up his assaults on all that is holy, as we draw nearer to the return of our Lord. This is no time for us to be unacquainted with the Scriptural witness regarding the devil and his wiles. And it is no time for us to be unaware of the great overcoming power that is ours through Jesus Christ.

This book examines four basic attacks of satan – afflictions, storms, temptations, and low self worth, and gives powerful insight into the tactics he uses to ensnare and defeat God's people.

It also examines what Scripture has to say in regard to our victory over those attacks.

Lastly, we list, at the end of each chapter, *"Principles to Remember"*, and relevant *Scripture verses*, that can help you stay focused and bring you through to victory, as you map out your Bible-based strategy against him.

* * * * * * * * * *

Between the covers of this book, you will find much wisdom from the Word of God, and a working knowledge of the principles of spiritual warfare gained from one who has been a "living, breathing battleground" – an arena where the forces of Good and the forces of Evil have regularly clashed in spiritual combat.

I have lived daily in the tension that exists when spiritual crosscurrents are hard at work, each vying for victory in the life of one seemingly insignificant believer.

I have been blessed to see and participate in what many would call the "Greater Works" that Jesus said His disciples would do – and, on the other hand, my knees have buckled at the retaliatory rage that hell brought against me for those works.

> *The same battle exists for every believer – for every child of God who loves Jesus and desires to follow Him.*

The difference is in the degree of the battle; and the degree of the battle has a lot to do with how great a threat we pose to satan, and to his plans to thwart God's purposes in our world and set up his own counterfeit kingdom.

Generally speaking, if the battle in your life is fierce, the stakes are high. Satan is too masterful at warring to waste his time with "small potatoes".

If the call of God on your life is to impact the Kingdom of God in a significant way, be prepared for major assaults and overt satanic attacks.

> *But also be prepared for the Lord to show up in a big way to bring you through to victory!*

* * * * * * * * * *

Let me share with you my experience. My earliest childhood memory was of the Good Shepherd revealing Himself to me in a powerful manifestation of love and peace.

I was but a babe in my mother's arms that Christmas Eve, as our whole family stood to hear the reading of the Gospel, in that small Evangelical Lutheran Church in Saginaw, Michigan.

As I gazed past Rev. Eichorn, who had moved into the pulpit for the reading, my eyes focused on the large picture to the right of the very ornate altar.

It was a portrait of Jesus, the Good Shepherd, with a staff in one hand, and a little lamb clutched to His bosom in the other.

Suddenly, and without warning, not only did my position change, but my "perspective" as well – and forever.

No longer was I securely cradled in my mother's arms in the fourth row (pulpit side, of course), of that white frame church on the corner of Main and Elm Streets.

I had been mysteriously transported into the arms of the Shepherd. I became the lamb He clutched so tenderly and held so gently to His bosom – all this, in some ethereal plane, eons away from where the rest of my family remained.

As I snuggled closer to the One whose love flooded my whole being, I felt a peace and a joy beyond the capability of mere words to describe.

Every fiber of my being seemed to come alive to

His touch, and *from that point on, I not only knew that Jesus was real – I knew that I, in some wonderful and inextricable way, belonged to Him, forever.*

That early childhood theophany opened, for me, a doorway into the unseen realm, which would bring not only joy and glory into my life, but pain and suffering as well.

You see, satan hates it when we are close to Jesus. He hates the anointing and the revelation knowledge that come as a result.

As we become empowered by that relationship, the devil has less and less impact upon our lives – and he views us as "armed and dangerous". We have the same potential to decimate his kingdom as Jesus had, because the Greater One lives in us.

So, in essence, he puts a spiritual "contract" out on us – and the war is on!

* * * * * * * * * *

St. Paul experienced this. His "thorn in the flesh" was a "messenger of satan" sent to torment him. (II Corin. 12:2-10). In other words, satan realized the degree of revelation knowledge given to Paul, and he put a contract out on him.

But God allowed it, in order to keep Paul dependent on Him and on His grace. So, for the rest of Paul's life, he was #1 on satan's "speed-dial" – and the battle raged. But God's grace was sufficient for him every time, and he finished his "course on earth" in victory.

* * * * * * * * *

Over the years, my awareness of that active, spiritual realm around us, became heightened – even as most around me seemed oblivious to its existence.

Accordingly, I experienced major satanic attacks in my life. I know what works in the hard place, and I know what doesn't.

And, thankfully, I have come out of each battle testifying to the faithfulness of Jesus to deliver.

Every time!

I'm concerned today, because many who find themselves in the throes of satanic attack, cannot even seem to identify the devil's involvement and strategy, much less stand against him.

Issues seem to get more cloudy by the day, as the Scriptural witness regarding the adversary and his diabolical schemes, is lost to a generation who attributes any discussion of satan and his wiles to be outdated, unsophisticated, and irrelevant to 21st century experience.

Satan does his best work, it seems,
when he can get us to believe
that he doesn't exist.

This book was written, not only to help you identify the wiles and strategies of the devil as he comes against the plans of God and His people, but to give you hope in the midst of <u>your</u> battles, as we present overcoming strategies and principles that brought victory into the lives of God's people historically.

* * * * * * * * * *

As we study, in detail, the temptation of Jesus in the wilderness, we glean "Five Key Strategies" that brought about His stunning victory over the devil.

These same strategies will bring you victory today in your battle, as you stand against his attacks.

We will also compare Jesus' battle strategy to that of Adam and Eve, and see why they failed so decisively in their time of testing.

This book is written that you might experience the same victory that Jesus enjoyed, using the same principles that He employed.

May you gather courage and hope and "overcoming power" as you read this book.

Phyllis Rawlins

Chapter One

Surviving the Fires
of Affliction

Surviving the Fires of Affliction

Affliction Is A Universal Experience

No one likes affliction and no one wants it to come their way. But like it or not, sooner or later we find ourselves face to face with trouble. We don't even have to go looking for it; it finds us.

It makes no difference what country we live in, how much money we make, or what our personal belief systems happen to be; no one is immune to affliction. It is one of the great common denominators of life, and no one who lives any length of time manages to escape its grasp. Affliction is the universal experience of the living.

Consider the testimony of the Bible regarding trouble:

> *Man is born to trouble as surely as sparks fly upward.*
> *(Job 5:7 RSV).*

*Man born of woman is of few days and
full of trouble.*
> *(Job14:1 RSV).*

*Each day has enough trouble of its
own.*
> *(Matt. 6:34b NIV).*

In this world you will have trouble.
> *(John 16:33b NIV).*

The Bible makes it clear that trouble and affliction are not occasional episodes in the lives of men, but rather, are common occurances, which ultimately touch the lives of every human being on Planet Earth.

*Perhaps you are presently experiencing trouble
and that has prompted your interest in this booklet.*

If so, I have good news for you!

*God wants to give you revelation today that will
help you win this battle!*

He has a devil-bustin', flame-quenchin' strategy
that will carry you out of the fire and into victory!

You <u>can</u> win at spiritual warfare!

Read on.

Affliction – What is it? And Can It Actually Serve A Good Purpose?

Webster's New Collegiate Dictionary defines affliction as "the state of being afflicted; the cause of continued pain of body or mind, as illness, loss, etc.; also "a grievous distress".

Often used synonyms include trial, tribulation, visitation, cross, torment, torture, adversity, calamity, distress, catastrophe, crisis, trouble, hardship, pressure and spiritual warfare.

You can see from the above list, which is not even exhaustive, that affliction can cover a lot of ground, and can be defined by the use of many related words.

And why not? It's been around since the Garden of Eden and the Fall of Man. Mankind has had a lot of time throughout history to ponder the "whys and wherefores" of affliction. And today, faced with our own perplexing experiences of trouble, each of us still must find for ourselves answers that satisfy and truths that bring victory.

Can fiery trials really serve any divine purpose in our lives?

What comfort can we find when we feel defeated and everything seems out of control?

How exactly do we survive the fires of affliction?

For the answer to these important questions we turn to expert testimony from one of the world's most experienced warriors for God. This historical Biblical figure not only struggled with great adversity, he found purpose in it, and ultimately was victorious through it.

If <u>he</u> did it, so can you.

David – A Man After God's Own Heart

In the year 1040 B.C., a son was born to Jesse of Bethlehem. He was the youngest of eight sons to be exact, and had two half-sisters as well.

Although David had a humble beginning as a shepherd boy who cared for his father's sheep, he persevered through various trials and afflictions in his lifetime to become the greatest king Israel had ever known.

Along with Moses, he is one of the two most prominent figures in the whole of Old Testament history.

Let's see what truths we can glean from David's life experience that can help us in our times of trial.

David's trouble really began after the prophet Samuel secretly anointed him to be Israel's future king. Saul, who occupied the throne at that time, had fallen out of favor with God because of his pride and disobedience. Consequently, God rejected him as king and chose David as his successor.

As David grew in godly character under the anointing, God began to exalt him and bring him into notoriety. As a teenager, Saul periodically summoned David to court to play his harp. So anointed was the music David played, that it was the only thing that soothed King Saul as he began the dark descent into demon possession.

David was also known as a brave young warrior, and even in his pre-adult years it was said of him that "the Lord is surely with him". (1 Sam. 16:18b).

Saul began to depend on David, and pressed David's father to allow him to be one of his armor-bearers. While still in his teens, David gained national acclaim after slaying the Philistine giant, Goliath, (1 Sam.17:45-47), in a daring feat of faith and courage. David even gained the loyalty and friendship of Saul's eldest son, Jonathan. Scripture says Jonathan "loved him as himself". (1 Sam. 18:1).

With David's popularity on the rise, Saul became increasingly jealous of David's prowess as a warrior. Accustomed to much adulation himself, it irked Saul when the crowds began to sing, *"Saul has slain his thousands and David his tens of thousands".* (1 Sam. 18:7).

For a man who was used to being in the center of attention, it was a tough blow. Saul feared David would seize the kingdom from him, spurred on by popular demand. From that point on, Saul purposed in his heart to kill young David.

In the next 12 years, David, already anointed to be king, became a hunted man. Imagine the irony. He was a fugitive on the run. Saul attempted to kill him no less than twenty one times.

* * * * * * * * * *

What had David done wrong to find
himself in such trouble?

Nothing. Absolutely Nothing.

*It wasn't what David had done wrong that got
him into the fire; it was what he had done right.*

* * * * * * * * * *

David had honored his God and his king in every way he knew how. He had developed a servant's heart over the years that he tenderly cared for his father's sheep. He developed a deep relationship with God as he worshipped Him with songs of praise. The Lord so loved David that He said of him, "He is a man after my own heart", (I Sam. 13:14), and He knew David could be trusted to lead His people with honor and selflessness.

> *Again, it wasn't what David did wrong that qualified him for this adversity – it was what he did right.*

* * * * * * * * * *

For years when I found myself in various trials and adversities, I would agonize over the question, "What have I done wrong?" "Where did I miss it?"

Finally, I had to learn to silence the "accuser of the brethren" when he came to condemn me and to bring me into despair.

I had to go back to the Word and read and re-read what it had to say about trouble, until I got it in my spirit. Jesus said, "In this world you will have tribulation" (trials and troubles).

Usually, it wasn't what I had done wrong that brought adversity upon me. Trouble is, simply, part of the reality of life, especially if we are endeavoring to follow Jesus.

The god of this world is mighty at laying snares to trap God's people, but God is <u>Almighty</u> in delivering us!

David wrote, *"Many are the afflictions of the righteous, but the Lord delivers him from them all."* *(Ps. 34:19 RSV).*

So take care, not to allow the devil to accuse and condemn you when you face various trials. Nine times out of ten, it's not what you've done <u>wrong</u> that has brought the trial; it's what you've done right.

When the enemy sees that you're moving forward for God, growing in faith, maturing in character, reaching for your destiny, those are prime times for him to attack.

- *He wants to break your focus.*
- *He wants to hinder you from reaching your goal.*
- *He wants you to walk away from your blessing – to give up on the promise.*
- *He wants to frighten and discourage you to the degree that you quit.*

You see, he knows a truth that is often hidden from us in stressful times – namely, that if you "keep on keeping on", you can't lose. God says so.

In fact, he knows that *the only way you won't gain the victory and come out of your situation more blessed than you went in, is if you quit.*

<u>Let me say it again.</u>
<u>The only way you lose is if you quit!</u>

David knew that, and so he persevered 12 long years in the desert, running for his life, but all the time trusting and believing that God would do what He promised. God used David's wilderness experience to fine-tune his leadership style, and later on, to build a rough and ready band of warriors who had a remarkable loyalty, and trust in the future king.

In spite of all the stresses and difficulties David faced daily, he didn't give up. He didn't quit. He "encouraged himself in the Lord" when he felt he couldn't go on, and God sustained him and brought him through the fire to victory!

AND WHAT A VICTORY IT WAS!

- Later, when David was crowned King of Israel and enjoyed the cheers and adulation of the crowds –

Do you think he questioned whether it had all been worth it?

- Later, when he surveyed the massive treasury of the Kingdom at his disposal –

Do you think he wished that he had quit the fight earlier?

- Later, when God crowned him with success unequaled by any other in that day –

Do you think David thought the price he paid was too great?

- Later, when David extended the borders of his kingdom from Egypt all the way to the Euphrates –

Do you think he had a revelation of why the battle had been so long and so hard?

- Later, when God promised that David's throne would endure forever and ever –

Do you think he regretted having stayed in the hard place all those years, forging out an intimate relationship with the One who causes kingdoms to rise and fall?

* * * * * * * * * *

David learned that the greater the battle, the greater the victory – and usually the more there is at stake.

* * * * * * * * * *

But I'm convinced he didn't learn that until after he won the victory of those many years in the wilderness. When he trudged through the hard places struggling with weariness and doubt, frustration and fear, he only had the promise of victory – but by God's grace, he kept his heart right, believed the promise, kept on praising and endured.

I wonder how many times you and I have lost the battle when victory lie just ahead. We took our eyes off of the promise, stopped praying over the prophecy, wearied in our well-doing, gave in to temptation, removed ourselves prematurely from the hard place, and just plain "caved in" before we got the victory.

We'll never know what was all at stake.

But we can learn from our mistakes. We can pick up the pieces and go on, and we can develop a strategy for use the next time the battle rages.

We can learn to be strong, and we can live free of condemnation, buoyed by the Lord's incredible kindness to those who fail –

And we can live to fight another day –

And We Can Win!

Just because you may have lost a battle at some point, doesn't mean you can't still win the war.

God promises to bring us through to victory if we'll just trust Him and stay in the battle until He wins it for us.

Romans 8:28 says, *"And we know that in all things God works for the good of those who love Him, who have been called according to His purpose"*. (NIV).

David certainly would give testimony to this

truth!

Do you know that it was during those difficult years, when David was struggling to hang on to the promise of his destiny, and having to fight daily for his life, that he penned most of the Psalms?

In the same way, most of the New Testament was written by Paul when he was a prisoner for Jesus Christ.

If John the Apostle had not been banished to the Isle of Patmos – and forcibly taken out of the mainstream of life in the first century A.D., would we have the powerful Revelation concerning the end times as part of New Testament canon today?

It is a truth that the hardest times in our lives are often the most productive.

Certainly adversity has a way of helping us to know what is important and what is not.

David wrote in Psalm 119, *"Before I was afflicted I went astray, but now I obey your word."* (vs. 67). *"It was good for me to be afflicted so that I might learn your decrees".* (vs. 71). *"The law from your mouth is more precious to me than thousands of pieces of silver and gold".* (vs. 72).

It was because of the relationship that David forged with God and His Word, and the lessons he learned, as he allowed God to shape his character in the wilderness, that God could later trust David with the glory that was to come.

* * * * * * * * * *

Do you think that David could have been entrusted with the bulging coffers of Israel if he had not first learned the real and greater value of eternal things?

Notice, that God was qualifying David for great prosperity as he stayed focused and faithful in the midst of lack.

Friend, what might God be qualifying you for in the midst of your present adversity?

* * * * * * * * * *

It was while David was constantly on the move to avoid being apprehended by Saul's armies, that he learned to trust God for his very life and freedom. So intense was Saul's jealousy and hatred for him, that David was forced to depend continually on God for guidance, provision, and protection.

In a very real way, it was in this difficult decade of his life that David learned how to be a sheep. He learned to follow as hard after God, as his father's sheep had once learned to follow after him.

You see, before you can be a shepherd,
You must first be a sheep.

I believe there are many in ministry today who have been catapulted into the limelight by self promotion, and set in office by man; who have not spent the necessary time in the wilderness of solitude and affliction, in order that God might forge them into vessels of honor. So don't be in too big of a hurry to get to the easy place. The truly valuable lessons of life are almost all learned in the hard place.

When we understand God's continued faithfulness to us – even in the furnace of affliction, even when there is no one else we can depend on – we can still rest peacefully, trusting our Good Shepherd to lead us through. That's what David did.

Oftentimes, until calamity and hardship invade our comfort zones, we focus on wrong priorities. We "major on the minors".

Corrie Ten Boom, the remarkable Christian who, along with her sister, suffered in Nazi prison camps because they hid Jewish people in their home, knew much about adversity. She said it this way, *"I fear we are often guilty of straightening pictures on the walls of houses that are burning with people trapped inside"*.

Adversity will give us a perspective on life that we didn't have before, and it will give a depth to the human soul that nothing else will.

That was David's experience and David's testimony.

* * * * * * * * * *

The Arabs have a saying that's popular in that part of the world: "All sunshine makes a desert". (Anon.)

If we allow them to, tribulation and difficulty can rain sympathy and empathy into our lives that can then flow from us into the lives of those who are trapped in affliction.

I don't know about you, but when I'm in trouble, I look for the companionship and wisdom of those who have been in the battle, and those who have been in the trenches. They have credibility. They are seasoned veterans who have been in the hard place, and they instinctively know how to minister to others when tough times come.

They are survivors who are living testimonies to the truth that there is life after trouble – life after affliction, life after divorce, life after bankruptcy, life after persecution, life after rejection and heartbreak. And most of these survivors see the world and people very differently than those who have known little pain.

* * * * * * * * * *

I know this much, that *we often see things in the*

darkness that we can't see in the light – wonderful things, things hidden from view and blocked by the light of day.

So it is, when we have dark nights of the soul and gut-wrenching experiences that blind our eyes to hope and direction and purpose. If we will but stay calm and allow our eyes to re-focus, we will see blessings and wonders, even in the darkness.

When I was very young, I developed a love for the stars. Night after night, I could be found gazing steadily toward heaven. I was mesmerized by the way they twinkled in the nighttime sky. I would spend hours searching for the big and little dippers – and any other designs that I could find. To witness a shooting star was a spectacle that would keep me excited for a week!

Do you know that stars do not really come out just at night? In fact, they never really leave their prescribed orbits until they die, by burning up, falling and entering our atmosphere. They're in the sky all day long. We just can't see them in the light. Stars can only be seen in the dark.

It is the same with other things as well – fire-flies, for instance. I used to take a mason jar out at night and catch fireflies, just for the fun of it. My twin brother, Phillip, and I used to have "contests" to see who could catch the most. As a child, it seemed like one of the true joys of the summer, to go darting back and forth in the darkness – determined to get the best "catch".

We don't really notice fireflies in the daytime. They're still flitting around, to be sure, but because of the light of the sun, our vision and our perspective changes.

So you see, there are many wonders to behold in the darkness.

In the same way, *there are things that are plainly visible only in the furnace of affliction.*

It is there that a deeper trust in our loving Heavenly Father is forged. It is there that we truly appreciate having such a wonderful High Priest, who Himself, is well acquainted with affliction, and is no stranger to sorrow and rejection, hardship and reproach.

In the midst of our own difficulties, we can often see with more understanding and appreciation, a fuller measure of the sacrifice Jesus made for us on the cross.

* * * * * * * * * *

Like David, I have seen the faithfulness of God toward me in the hard place. I have discovered that He is actually drawn to us when we're in trouble – just like a moth to a flame. It is His very nature to save and deliver, even when we manage to get into difficulty because of our own mistakes.

So, when the devil turns up the heat and things begin to unravel, God is not concerned. He is not panicked. He is not worried. You see, He knows how faithful and trustworthy He is! And He knows that He has every ability to safely guide us to victory.

Psalm 78:72 says, *"So He led them according to the integrity of His heart; and guided them by the skillfulness of His hands". (KJV).*

In 1 Corinthians 10, Paul writes, *"There hath no temptation (test or trial) come upon you that is not common to man; but God is faithful, who will not suffer you to be tempted above what you are able; but will with the temptation (test or trial) also make a way to escape, that ye may be able to bear it".* (vs. 13 KJV).

And, at the end of the Apostle Peter's life, he penned the words, *"God surely knows how to rescue godly men from trials (tests and temptations)". (II Peter 2:9).*

Our God is an all-powerful, all-faithful, devil-bustin', fire-quenchin' Deliverer!

The good news is that God wants to show Himself strong on our behalf. He wants to capture our hearts, and gain our loyalty. So, when satan suddenly bursts onto the scene with his latest brand of treachery, God says, "O.K. devil. Bring it on. No matter what you do, I will turn it for their good".

God is so committed to our eternal welfare, that He misses no opportunity to move us to a position of deeper, more intimate fellowship with Him so that we will be stronger. He knows, you see, that when we are weak, we are really strong in Him, because He chooses to vest us, in the hard place, with the grace we need to carry us through to victory. We need only to go to Him in childlike trust and humility.

* * * * * * * * * *

We're like little children who often fall down and scrape our knees. It pleases God when we go running home to Him – home where we belong, home where He can pull us up on His lap and comfort us, home where He can wrap His tender arms around us, heal our hurts, and dry our tears, as He whispers:

> *"Fear not, little one, for I have redeemed you; I have called you by name, you are mine. When you pass through the waters, I will be with you; and when you pass through the rivers, they will not sweep over you. When you walk through the fire, you will not be burned; I promise you, the flames will not set you ablaze. For I am the Lord, your God, the Holy One of Israel, your Savior".*
> (Is. 43:1-3).

* * * * * * * * * *

The truth is, that God loves us so much, and longs so much for a deep and intimate relationship with us, that He is willing to allow us to go through difficult and painful experiences, if that is ultimately what will bring us to Him. I'm convinced, that He first tries, in many ways, to gently woo us to Himself by the Spirit.

But if His overtures of love go unheeded, He will allow the devil to intervene in our circumstances, in order that we recognize our helplessness and go running back to the only safe refuge there is – Him! In that way, *the devil is really just a tool that God uses at His good pleasure.*

In fact, everything that touches our lives is "Father-filtered" first – especially affliction. This is an important point. God monitors everything related to His children. Satan must get permission to bring any hardship into our lives. If God determines that we "qualify" to receive this affliction – meaning, He knows we have everything we need to endure it and to have victory over it – satan receives the "go-ahead". I believe that God monitors our faith level first, and every other weapon in our spiritual arsenal. When He is fully satisfied that victory is attainable, He gives satan permission to bait the trap.

If this were <u>not</u> so, how could God say in His Word:

*"But thanks be to God, who always
leads us and causes us to triumph..."*
(2 Cor. 2:14).

God's plan, then, is to carry us through the
battle into victory – and, "to the victor go the
spoils". It is God's intent to bless us. His motive in
all that He does, is love.

* * * * * * * * * *

Some years ago, I had the occasion to visit with
a shepherd. I was considering accepting a position
as Pastor of a rural congregation in Nebraska. The
Bishop of that district thought it advisable to fly me
there for a week-end interview. Several members of
the congregation had sheep.

What a learning experience!

One afternoon, as I walked the rolling hills with
this modern day shepherd, he shared with me a
practice that sheep herders in Palestine use in dealing with errant lambs:

Occasionally, a lamb is born into the sheepfold
and has a mind of its own. Usually these lambs are
careless and wander too far from the fold and from
the protection of the shepherd. After repeatedly
having to leave the rest of the sheep to go after the
little stray, the shepherd knows to do the only thing

that will ultimately save its life. *He breaks one of its legs!* Sound cruel? It seems so, but stay with me, now, for "the rest of the story".

The shepherd then begins to bandage the broken leg, talking gently to the lamb and stroking it, while he lovingly says words to this effect:

> *"You silly little lamb - don't you know there are wolves and lions out there who would love to have you for dinner? You are so small that you would only be a light snack for them. And if the lions and wolves didn't get you, there are rocky cliffs you could fall from, and snakes and pits and lots of other dangers as well. You are very precious to me, and I must teach you, in the only way I know how, to stay close".*

From that point on, the shepherd knows his little charge cannot keep up with the rest, so the shepherd must carry him until his leg is healed. He carries him in the crook of his left arm, so that, while nestled safely in the bosom of the shepherd, the little lamb can also experience the calming effect of the shepherd's heartbeat.

By the time his little leg is healed, there is such a bond between the two, that the lamb will never stray again.

* * * * * * * * * *

While I don't believe that our loving Heavenly Father goes around breaking the legs of His wayward people, He does allow us to experience the consequences of our own actions, By His permissive will, He also, at times, allows the enemy to trap us in the fires of adversity – all the while knowing that He has every intention and ability to turn things for our good as we look to Him in trust – and learn to know His heart.

* * * * * * * * * *

The Old Testament prophet, Zephaniah, truly captured the posture of our Father's heart toward us, when he wrote 600 years before the birth of Christ:

> *"The Lord your God is with you*
> *He is mighty to save.*
> *He takes great delight in you;*
> *He will quiet you with His love.*
> *He will rejoice over you with singing."*
> (Zeph. 3:17).

You just gotta love a Father who is so taken with us that He sings!

* * * * * * * * * *

So, the next time adversity comes, and darkness falls all around you, and fear presses in so hard that every breath is a struggle, just listen with your heart, and you are sure to hear a tender voice singing to you:

> *"Come child. Take my hand and don't be afraid. This is but part of the plan. Trust me, for in the fullness of time, when this affliction has done its work, I myself shall deliver you."*

Surviving The Fires of Affliction Principles to Remember

- *No one escapes affliction*, especially those endeavoring to live a Christian life.

- *God will meet you where you are, even in the fires of affliction, if you are seeking Him.* "A seeking heart and a seeking Savior always connect."

- *We must develop a basic plan of strategy that will give us direction in the times of adversity,* and carry us through to victory.

- *David found purpose in his afflictions* – and ultimately won the victory.

- *The greater the battle, the greater the victory* – and usually, the more there is at stake.

- *It isn't always what you've done wrong that lands you in the furnace of affliction*; sometimes it's what you've done right.

- *Do not Fear.* Fear is the opposite of faith – and it is faith that releases the promises of God.

FEAR is <u>F</u>alse <u>E</u>vidence <u>A</u>ppearing <u>R</u>eal.

Do not receive it.

- *The only way we can lose is if we quit.*

- *Satan's biggest onslaughts are usually in the homestretch of the race* – just before you are about to cross the finish line.

- *The devil is a liar and a thief who specializes in dream-stealing.*

- *If the enemy is failing in his efforts to stop you from reaching your goal, he will search for some-one close to you who will unknowingly serve as his pawn.*

- *God will turn all things for our good if we love Him – and trust Him in the battle.*

- *The hardest times in our lives are often the most productive.*

- *Adversity has a way of helping us sort out our priorities in life.*

- "All sunshine makes a desert." *God uses the rain to cause us to have sympathy toward others who are suffering.*

- *The devil is just a tool that God uses at His discretion and good pleasure.*

- *The Father quiets us with His love and joys over us with singing.* He will never leave us alone.

- *We are redeemed from the Curse of the Law* (poverty, sickness, and the second death) and we are Heirs of Abraham's Blessing – <u>*Never Forget That!*</u> (Gal. 3:13,14).

- Remember, *in Christ we have dominion over satan in our lives.* Stand against him in faith and command him to go.

- *Never admit defeat,* and never glorify the devil by speaking about the attacks he is bringing against you.

- Instead, *confess what the Word of God says about your situation and your victory.*

- *Give Glory and Praise to God!*

Surviving the Fires of Affliction

A Devil-bustin', Fire-quenchin' Strategy for Victory!

Any strategy that results in victory over the power of the enemy in your life must incorporate the following elements:

1) *Faith in Jesus Christ* as your personal Lord and Savior, healer, provider and deliverer. (If you have never asked Him into your heart and confessed Him as Lord and Savior, please refer to the "Prayer for Salvation" at the back of this book).

2) *A working and growing knowledge of the Word of God.* It is the only offensive weapon against the attacks of the devil. Speak the Word over yourself and your situation.

3) *A willingness to praise,* even when you don't feel like it. God inhabits the praises of His people. In other words, He comes and dwells in the midst of our praises. "If God is (with and) for us, who can be against us?" (Romans 8:31b).

4) *The determination to stand against fear* – which is the opposite of faith. Refuse to accept fear. Speak to it and command it to go

in Jesus' name.

5) *An awareness that the greatest battles of this war will be waged in your mind and on your lips.* Never admit defeat and never agree with the devil. Guard against thinking and speaking doubt, fear, and negativity. Do not murmur and complain. Give the devil no ground. Victory is won through your faith and a testimony that agrees with what God says.

6) *A willingness to separate yourself from dream-stealers and ungodly counselors* who speak words that destroy hope and cast dispersions on what God has promised you. Guard what you hear.

7) *A walk of obedience to God.* Sin blocks the flow of God's power and anointing in your life.

8) *A willingness to pray without ceasing.* Put yourself in the place of prayer so you can hear clearly as He reveals the battle plan for your victory.

9) *A willingness to enlist the support of seasoned prayer warriors* who know the Word of God, love the Lord, and who live accordingly.

10) *A willingness to fast* if the Lord directs you to do so. Prayer and fasting together are powerful weapons that tear down the strongholds of the enemy.

11) <u>*Continued Tithing.*</u> It is imperative that you live under an open heaven. God promises to rebuke the devourer when we are faithful in our giving.

12) <u>*Courage.*</u> You must be brave. You are not alone. Jesus is in the fire with you to sustain you and to deliver you. Trust Him and stay focused on Him. He shall not disappoint you.

If you will build your strategy based on these basic, but important elements, I promise you, you will not be in the fire long.

And you will not just survive the Fires of

Affliction; you will have victory in every way!

The Weapon of the Word to Help You
Survive the Fires of Affliction

(Read these verses out loud daily and meditate on them.)

"Many are the afflictions of the righteous; but the Lord delivers him out of them all."

(Ps. 34:19 RSV).

"Consider mine affliction, and deliver me; for I do not forget Thy law."
"... for the Lord hath comforted His people, and will have mercy upon His afflicted."

(Is. 49:13b KJV).

"In all their affliction He was afflicted, ... in His love and in His pity He redeemed them; and He bore them, and carried them all the days of old."

(Is. 63:9 KJV).

"... yea, in the shadow of Thy wings will I make my refuge, until these calamities be past."

(Ps. 57:16 KJV).

"But the Lord is faithful, who shall establish you and keep you from evil."
(II Thess. 3:3 KJV).

"... in all these things we are more than conquerors through Him that loved us."
(Rom. 8:37).

"... when the enemy shall come in like a flood, the Spirit of the Lord shall lift up a standard against him."
(Isa. 59:19b KJV).

"The Lord knoweth how to deliver the godly out of temptations (tests and trials), and to reserve the unjust unto the day of judgment to be punished."
(II Peter 2:9 KJV).

"God is our refuge and strength, a very present help in trouble."
(Ps. 46:1 KJV).

"Because thou hast made the Lord, which is my refuge, even the Most High, thy habitation; there shall no evil befall thee; neither shall any plague come nigh thy dwelling. For He shall give His angels charge over thee, to keep thee in all thy ways."
(Ps. 91:9-11 KJV).

Chapter Two

Riding Out the Storm –
On the Way to Your
Destiny

Riding Out the Storm – On the Way to Your Destiny

"Truth Revealed"
(Mark 4:1-20).

It was a destiny decision that brought Jesus to Galilee. It is where His ministry was to be headquartered. Its location was strategic. All the important trade routes in that part of the world passed through this northern-most province of Palestine.

The district boasted many cities with populations over 15,000, nine of which stood on the shores of the Sea of Galilee.

Accordingly, these cities of substance and size often hosted merchants and seamen from all over the world – travelers who came espousing a wide variety of different religions, dogmas, and ideas.

The people there were known to be friendly, liberal-minded, and almost always ready to converse and entertain new ideas and experiences.

What a perfect place for Jesus to begin His public ministry.

As His message and teachings took root there, they could easily be spread to the surrounding towns and villages – and even carried around the world.

What better place for Jesus to bring a new teaching regarding the Word of God than here?

* * * * * * * * * *

Now, Jesus knew how to capture the attention of a crowd. He was a storyteller par excellence. That morning, the method He used to stir the hearts of the listeners to a greater hunger for truth, was the "parable".

In fact, among his spirited teachings that day, He told several parables.

But the one He told first, the "Parable of the Sower", was the most important one. It was the one He emphasized the most, for it contained a truth so basic and so significant, that Jesus knew the disciples must thoroughly comprehend it, if they were to be successful in walking out their God-given destinies.

Slowly and distinctly, Jesus began:

"A sower went forth to sow; and when he sowed, some seeds fell by the wayside, and the birds came and devoured them.

"Some fell upon stony places, where they had not much earth; immediately they sprang up, because they had no deepness of earth.

"And when the sun was up, they were scorched; and because they had no root, they withered away.

"And some fell among thorns; and the thorns sprang up, and choked them.

"But others fell into good ground, and brought forth fruit; some an hundred-fold, some sixty-fold,

some thirty-fold.
"He who has hears to hear, let him hear."
                                        (Mark 4:3b-9).

It was only later, in private, and in response to the disciples' questions about the parable, that Jesus clearly interpreted it.

He likened the Sower to Himself, and the Seed as being the Word of God. The various types of ground that the seed fell on were representative of the hearts of the hearers.

Jesus then told them, the disciples, that they were blessed, and had been chosen to know the secrets of the Kingdom.

As Jesus explained the hidden truths of the parable, He went into a lengthy discourse on the tactics that satan uses to steal the "seed" – or rather, to steal the "Word of the Lord", from men's hearts and lives.

He talked about hardness of hearts, trials, persecutions, the pressure and cares of daily living, worldliness, the deceitfulness of riches, and the lust of other things.

I'm not sure that the disciples understood the importance, just then, of what Jesus was telling them, but they surely would later.

In fact, this teaching would be of paramount importance to them before that very day was over – for they were soon to experience a lesson so extraordinary that they would never forget it.

* * * * * * * * * *

"An Extraordinary Lesson"

It seemed like a reasonable request, although "request" is hardly the proper word to describe the Master's command to "Go over to the other side". After all, it wasn't as if He left any room for objection as He cast His gaze toward the eastern shore. He was tired. Bone-weary.

He had spent the entire day confined to a well-worn fishing vessel moored just off the shore of the Sea of Galilee. It was a day of teaching and instruction.

No one relished opportunities such as this, more than Jesus. In fact, His servant's heart often drove Him to minister to the hurting masses far beyond what His physical strength would allow.

Tonight, He was operating on the strength of sheer endurance alone.

All in all, it had been a long, but successful campaign. Never before, had Jesus seen such crowds pressing Him. Never before, had He sensed such a hunger and such need – and such an opportunity to share the Father's love.

As the word spread that the Healer was in town, the crowds grew larger and larger, until earlier that morning, Jesus had been forced to climb into a boat, cast out from the water's edge, and continue teaching from there.

In the crowd were some from Judea and some from Jerusalem. Others gathered, who had traveled from Tyre and Sidon – and from practically all the surrounding towns and villages.

Each, in their own way, had made the effort to be in the press of the crowd that day.

Some, were driven by need and by the knowledge that they had no where else to go. They unashamedly cried out to Jesus, and pushed their way closer and closer to the One who could do the impossible.

The demon possessed found themselves suddenly prostrate before Him, as evil spirits were forced, by the sheer power of His anointing, to acknowledge He who had authority – even over the kingdom of darkness.

No, never before had the crowds seen anything like it. Blind eyes opened! Lepers cleansed! The deaf suddenly able to hear! And once belligerent spirits now crying out for mercy!

* * * * * * * * * *

Jesus was a show-stopper, to be sure. All that power and authority wrapped up in the form of One who looked surprisingly like them – who would have ever thought … ?

His touch was gentle, His smile compelling, His ways, beyond winsome – and His concern and compassion surpassed anything ever experienced by these common folk.

No wonder they followed Him from place to place.

No wonder they left their homes and businesses to tag after this nomadic Galilean whom fate, they were convinced, had sent their way.

No wonder they gathered that day on the breezy shore and hung on His every word.

* * * * * * * * *

But now, the sun was setting. The day was quite spent, and so was Jesus.

As He felt the ship get underway, He doggedly made His way to the rear of the craft.

There He curled up on the only cushion He could find on board. Hardly a feather pillow and a down comforter, but it would do.

"Rest", He murmured to Himself, "I just need a little rest.".

Had He had the strength, had it been a less taxing day, had the crowds been smaller, the needs not as pronounced, had the energy He expended been less, Jesus could have easily walked to the other side. It was only twelve miles.

But when one is in the grip of that kind of all-encompassing exhaustion, twelve feet would have seemed too far to walk … and what of the lingering crowds still on the shore who would not be denied?

Clearly, this was the only place of rest and solitude the Master could find.

* * * * * * * * * *

Who knows how long that sturdy craft floated along in relative ease before the wind began to blow with hurricane force?

Who knows how close to its destination that vessel actually came, before the waves sloshed over the sides of the boat and threatened to wash them overboard?

Who knows how long Peter and Andrew, and Zebedee's sons – all crusty tars of the sea, waited and bailed, and tried to handle the situation themselves, before they reached the point of desperation?

After all, they were veteran seamen who made their living fishing on these waters. They knew the sea, and they knew their boat. And they knew themselves.

They knew their prowess in out-maneuvering whatever storms had raged against them in the past, and that their skill had always seen them through.

And they knew each other, too, and that they could work effectively as a team, handling that which they didn't dare face alone – namely the unpredictability of that particular body of water.

You see, the Sea of Galilee often boasted of violent storms.

To be sure, one didn't last long as a fisherman on that sea unless he was not only highly skilled in navigating rough waters, but also courageous enough to handle the unexpected and still keep his wits about him.

* * * * * * * * *

It probably seemed like business as usual, as they set sail that evening for the distant shore.

As they confidently and calmly navigated the familiar waters before them, *little did they know that a mighty storm of mighty proportions was already brewing on the horizon...*And that the storm about to bear down on them would be so severe that they would not be able to save themselves ...

Little did they know, that in a matter of just a few moments, their serenity would turn to desperation, their confidence would turn to hopelessness, and Death would draw very near.

And little did they know, that the age-old enemy of men's souls, had masterminded the soon coming crisis in a well-planned scheme to kill them all.

Little did they know ...

* * * * * * * * *

I wonder whose idea it was to finally wake the sleeping Savior. Surely, they held out as long as they could.

These were strong and prideful men – prideful in their ability to handle every situation that confronted them.

It would not be easy for them to swallow their pride, admit defeat, confess their fear, and come to Jesus.

But here they were, fresh out of strength, fresh out of ideas, fresh out of hope, and fresh out of luck–

And only minutes away from death and disaster.

En masse, the terrified disciples roused the resting Jesus, and cried, "Master, don't You care if we perish?"

How like human nature to try everything first before going to the Lord.

How like human nature it is, to wait until things get completely out of control, before we cry out to the only One who can be our Sure Anchor in the storm.

We have a way of neglecting Him when the seas are calm. When the sailing is smooth and we have a feeling of mastery over our circumstances, we hardly give a thought to the One who is the real Master of our Destiny.

Oh, but when the storm hits, and the wind howls, and the waves threaten to undo us – when our boats begin to rock so wildly that we can't seem to hold on; then, like the disciples, we remember that Jesus is on board our ship.

And, surely, no ship with the Savior on board could ever sink ..... or could it?

The disciples were soon to find out.

* * * * * * * * * *

Had the disciples mistaken Jesus' slumber for unconcern with their plight?

Had His deep sleep rendered Him unconscious of their need, and therefore unable or unwilling to help?

Whatever their thinking, whatever might have been their hesitation in calling on the Master sooner, they must have been greatly relieved and awed, when He promptly arose, addressed the elements by name, and stilled the storm.

> *"He rebuked the wind and said to the sea, "Hush now!" And the wind ceased and sank to rest as if exhausted by its beating, and there was immediately a great calm and a perfect peacefulness."*
>
> (Mark 4:39 AMP).

* * * * * * * * * *

How very kind of the Savior to deliver the disciples from danger first, before He tackled the weighty issues of fear and faith – and, no doubt, reiterated to them the teaching of earlier that day. He waited until the winds were calm and the sea was smooth, and the disciples were somewhat quieted, before He sternly rebuked them for their fear and the littleness of their faith.

As the disciples mellowed out and became cognizant of Jesus' mastery over the elements and His authority over nature, their knees must have buckled at the wonder of what they had just seen.

"Who is this?", they marveled, "that even the wind and the waves obey Him?"

(Mark 4:41b).

* * * * * * * * * *

On the Way to <u>Your</u> Destiny

*Do you know what lies between you and the
fulfilling of your destiny?*

STORMS!

*The Bible (and history) is brimming with the
stories of men and women of destiny who encoun-
tered various storms as they walked
out the will of God for their lives.*

* * * * * * * * *

<u>David</u>

Take David, for instance. Between the time the
Prophet Samuel anointed him to be the King of
Israel, and the time he actually ascended the throne,
he spent twelve years running for his life in the
wilderness, as Saul, enraged by jealousy, attempted
to have him assassinated. There were no less than
twenty-one attempts on David's life.

*You want to talk "storms"? David
knew some things about experiencing
storms on the way to his destiny.*

Joseph

Joseph was another man of destiny who knew what it was to be in the hard place.

As a child, he had prophetic dreams. But, the jealousy of his brothers, and the favoritism showed him by his father, led to his being sold into slavery in Egypt.

But God prospered him, even in that situation.

One day, his master's wife attempted to seduce Joseph, but he resisted temptation, and rejected her advances.

Angry at being scorned, Potifar's wife concocted a false story, and Potifar had Joseph imprisoned. He remained there for many years.

But God continued to bless him even in prison, and he was placed in a leadership position over all the other prisoners.

Eventually, Joseph was released by Pharaoh, when he was found to be the only one who could interpret the King's prophetic dream.

The King made him the head of the royal granaries. He was second in command in the whole of Egypt – answerable only to Pharaoh.

His instrumentation of a new program of saving and dispensing Egypt's mighty resources, based on the warnings in Pharaoh's dream, saved the day, when several years later, famine hit.

Not only was Egypt prepared, but it prospered because of Joseph's God-given wisdom. Many other countries were saved from starvation as well, as they came to Egypt to buy grain. *Among those seeking to do business were Joseph's brothers.*

God used Joseph to sustain his own family, and to save his own people, thus, preserving their lineage. It was out of that lineage, centuries later, that the Messiah would come.

> *Joseph literally went from the prison to the palace, but not without some hardships, some time, and some storms in between.*

Paul

Paul, the great missionary to the Gentiles, received a "destiny word" that he was to go to Rome to stand trial before Caesar.

But a furious storm raged against the ship that he was on, and, had it not been for the wisdom of Paul – and God's favor upon him – all 276 on board would have been killed.

Ultimately, Paul arrived in Rome, and while he waited for two years for his accusers to put together their case against him, he preached the Gospel to all who would listen.

Paul stayed on course with his destiny, but had to ride out a storm and a ship-wreck to do it.

* * * * * * * * * *

In each of these cases, furious squalls in the form of storms, trials, and adversities, came upon these men *after* they had received a destiny word from God, and *directly after* they stepped out in faith and in obedience to that word.

The unforeseen events that followed, were not from God.

On the contrary, these "storms" were attacks of the devil. Satan wanted to blow these men off course, by getting their attention focused on circumstances rather than on their established destinies.

He tried to steal the word – the promise – from their hearts.

But God was faithful, and brought each of them through to their "appointed end".

* * * * * * * * * *

In the same way, in the account of the "Stilling

of the Storm", Jesus had just given the disciples a destiny Word – a directional Word, "Let us go over to the other side".

It was as they stepped out in obedience to that command, that a "furious storm of hurricane proportions", blew upon them.

> *Now some storms happen in life due to natural causes – one force in nature colliding with another.*

> *But this was no ordinary storm.*

The disciples were used to ordinary storms. They knew how to handle them. No, this storm was outside of the ordinary –or "supernatural" in origin, and in ferocity.

The Greek word "megas" is used in Scripture to describe this squall. We get our word "mega" or "mighty" from this word. In other words, a mighty or "mega"storm blew up quickly.

Accordingly, we can recognize satan's attacks against us by the following characteristics:

1) *The storm comes after you receive a destiny word from God.*

2) *The storm blows up quickly and with no advance warning.* You don't usually see it coming until it's too late.

3) *The storm is always epidemic in proportion.* The devil specializes in over-kill. It's not just a storm, it's a "mega-storm". It's not just one thing that goes wrong, it's ten!

4) *The impact of the storm leaves you "reeling", feeling "adrift", and wondering where you went wrong, and if God is trying to tell you something.*

(Psssst! He is! He's trying to tell you, "You're under attack!" So, "Batten down the hatches, hold on to the promise, and trust Me – I'll carry you through!").

* * * * * * * * *

The intent of these storms is to get you to veer off course – to change your mind – to doubt God's plan for your life – or to jump ship altogether!

* * * * * * * * *

Remember, the devil is a murderer, a thief, and a liar. He specializes in killing dreams and stealing destinies.

Jesus said so!

* * * * * * * * *

73

In order to be successful, he must find a way to separate you from the Word – the Written Word of God (the Logos), and the "Rhema" Word that you have been given. (A "rhema" word is a specific word that God has quickened to your spirit by His Spirit).

Storms can have that impact if we are not careful.

They are meant to hinder our journey
and interrupt our faith walk.

They are "fear-inducers" –
and fear is the opposite of faith.

Fear is, actually, faith in the enemy.

* * * * * * * * * *

God tells us in His Word, that He has not "*given us a spirit of fear, but of power, love, and a sound mind*".

(II Tim. 1:7).

Fear will never allow the release of the promises of God in your life. His promises manifest only as you take hold of them by faith.

Fear will stop you in your tracks, and

> *it will empower satan to hinder and harass you even more.*

That's why Jesus rebuked the disciples so strongly when they roused Him from His slumber on the boat.

It wasn't the fact that they woke Him that brought a rebuke. It was the fact that they were operating in FEAR. Jesus knew where that spirit had come from, and discerned that the devil had already been at work, laying a snare for them – attempting to steal His word from their hearts.

Fear and doubt go hand-in-hand, and the disciples were expressing both.

In actuality, the disciples had the authority on the basis of the Master's word, ("Let us go over to the other side"), to stand up in faith and rebuke the storm themselves.

But they were ignorant of their own spiritual power, and ignorant of satan's involvement in this whole scenario. Therefore, they caved in to his deception. They didn't stand against him. They cowered in fear.

* * * * * * * * * *

You see,

The disciples were not the only ones desperate in that situation. Actually, satan, himself, was desperate, but they didn't know that.

Let me tell you why:

There was a certain demon-possessed man on the other shore, crying in the tombs – and satan did not want to lose this hell-bound captive! Jesus had already decimated his kingdom enough.

But God, in His mercy, had arranged a divine appointment with The Deliverer, for this tormented soul. Help was on the way. Jesus was coming to the rescue.

Satan knew he had to keep the two of them apart, if he wanted to keep his "prey" bound – and he already had his plan in place:

"I'll just blow up a little storm, the likes of which they've never seen before – and I'll do it while "He" sleeps. Ha-ha."

"What "He" doesn't know won't hurt Him …. much."

Satan must have rubbed his filthy, blood-stained hands together with glee, at seeing these rookie disciples so vulnerable, and so afraid.

If he could only destroy their ship and all on board, he would reign supreme. No one would ever again dare to contest his dominion.

"But", the devil reasoned fiendishly, "there is only a small window of opportunity."

He had to catch the disciples off guard, intimidate them by the severity of the storm. And he had to do it while Jesus took His rest. "It's the only chance I have," he sneered knowingly.

"Ah, but not to worry", he reassured himself.

"Things are proceeding nicely. A little more wind ... a little more water sloshing over the sides ... and it will soon be over ...".

How cunning ... how perfectly timed ... how fiendishly evil ...

By his estimation, it was a fool proof plan. (Need I say, dear reader, that the operative word here is "Fool!).

Obviously, satan either underestimated the willingness of Jesus to come to the rescue of the disciples, or perhaps he just didn't believe that Jesus had the power and the authority to control the forces of nature – after all, Jesus was in "human form", now.

Whatever his miscalculation that day, he was sorely defeated as Jesus asserted His legal authority as Sovereign Lord of All.

I'd like to think that there was one that day, whose knees were weaker than the disciples' knees, after witnessing the spectacle of Jesus' power – namely, satan, who was utterly foiled, and thus forced to abandon, until a more opportune time, his plan for the destruction of them all.

What an awesome learning experience for the disciples.

* * * * * * * * * *

- *No doubt, they would pay stricter attention to the teachings of Jesus from now on.*

- *No doubt, they learned that they could trust Jesus, even in the toughest storms of life.*

- *No doubt, they understood in a deeper way, the awesome Sovereignty of their Lord.*

- *No doubt, they understood more clearly the seriousness of the devil's plans against them all.*

- *No doubt, they understood as never before, that no matter how devious the devil's plans, no matter how well executed and how quickly those plans might arise, satan was no match for their Messiah.*

- *And, no doubt, to them, knowing this truth made the whole extraordinary experience worth it all.*

* * * * * * * * * *

Friends, be assured that once the wind dies down in your storm – and the waves retreat to normal size, you, too, will know many things that you could only learn in the place of the storm.

* * * * * * * * * *

As You Ride Out the Storm – Principles to Remember

- *No storm lasts forever.* This is a temporary situation. There is an end to it, even if you can't see it. "Out-endure" the enemy.

- *Resist fear.* Speak to it. Command it to go. Speak out the Word of God and His promises to you.

- *Don't jump ship.* Keep on "keeping on: You must be headed in the right direction, or else, "why the attack"?

- *Just because Jesus is "on board" doesn't make you immune to attacks.* Sometimes the attacks happen precisely because He is "on board". But He will see you through to victory if you will trust Him.

- *No ship sinks when Jesus is on it.* It may rock back and forth and get tossed to and fro, but it will stay afloat if you stay focused on Him and follow His directions.

- *After a great storm, there will always be an equally great calm.*

- *There is always a risk involved to following your*

destiny. It takes faith and courage, *but it will be worth it all.*

- *Stay in regular communication with Jesus.* Don't wait until things are out of control before communicating to Him your need.

- *The only sure anchor that will hold in a mega-storm is Jesus.*

- *The storm is not your destination* – the "opposite shore" is, where there are works for you to do that have been established from before the foundation of the world.

- *Jesus wants you to reach your destiny more than you do.*

- *Never let a storm determine your destiny.* Your destiny is established by God.

- *Never doubt in the storm, what God has told you in the calm.*

- *Take your cues from Jesus.* He knew who He was, and where He was going, so He could rest confidently, in the midst of the storm.

- *Stay in God's Word, so your "joy level" will be high.* "The joy of the Lord is our strength" – and we need strength to win the battle.

Joy produces strength which produces victory.

- *Be thankful to God in the midst of the storm.*
  - How else would we know how much we can trust Jesus?
  - How else would we know how mighty He is to save?
  - How else could we minister to others in the midst of their storms?

- *God has everything under control.* He's a big God who can do big things.

He'll help you "ride out the storm" to victory, "on the way to your destiny".

The Weapon of the Word to Help You Ride Out the Storm

(Speak these verses out loud daily and meditate on them.)

"They cried unto the Lord in their trouble, and He delivered them out of their distresses."

(Ps. 107:6).

"For I, the Lord thy God, will hold thy right hand, saying unto thee, Fear not; I will help thee."

(Isa. 41:13).

"Now thanks be unto God, which always causeth us to triumph in Christ …"

(II Cor. 2:14a KJV).

"… For this purpose the Son of God was manifested, that He might destroy the works of the devil".

(I John 3:8b).

"He hath delivered my soul in peace, from the battle that was against me …"

(Ps. 55:18 KJV).

"Yea, though I walk through the valley of the

shadow of death, I will fear no evil; for Thou are with me; thy rod and thy staff they comfort me."

(Ps. 23:4 KJV).

"… But they that seek the Lord shall not want any good thing."

(Ps. 34:10 KJV).

"I sought the Lord, and He heard me, and delivered me from all my fears."

(Ps. 34:4 KJV).

" The Name of the Lord is a strong tower; the righteous run into it and are safe."

(Prov. 18:10).

"For God hath not given us the spirit of fear; but of power, and of love, and of a sound mind."

(II Tim. 1:7).

"Being confident of this very thing; that He which hath begun a good work in you will perform it until the day of Jesus Christ."

(Phil. 1:6 KJV).

"Casting all your care upon Him; for He careth for you."

(I Pet. 5:7 KJV).

Chapter Three

Dealing With
Double-Edged Temptations

Dealing With
Double Edged Temptations

"The Nature of the Tempter"

Martin Luther, the great church reformer, once spent the better part of a year hiding out in the Wartburg Castle in Germany. It was there, in relative solitude and safety, that he translated the New Testament into the German language. It is also widely purported that he wrote his most famous hymn, "A Mighty Fortress Is Our God", from that place of refuge.

In this hymn, Luther gives voice to the battle that rages in this world between the Creator and His adversary:

> A mighty fortress is our God,
> A sword and shield victorious;
> He breaks the cruel oppressor's rod
> And wins salvation glorious.
> The old satanic foe
> Has sworn to work us woe!
> With craft and dreadful might
> He arms himself to fight,
> On earth he has no equal.
>
> No strength of ours can match his might!

We would be lost, rejected.
But now a champion comes to fight,
Whom God Himself elected.
You ask who this may be?
The Lord of Hosts is He!
Christ Jesus, mighty Lord,
God's only Son, adored.
He holds the field victorious.

Though hordes of devils fill the land
All threat'ning to devour us.
We tremble not, unmoved we stand,
They cannot overpow'r us.
Let this world's tyrant rage;
In battle we'll engage!
His might is doomed to fail'
God's judgment must prevail!
One little Word subdues him.

God's Word forever shall abide,
No thanks to foes who fear it!
For God Himself fights by our side
With weapons of the Spirit.
Were they to take our house,
Goods, honor, child, or spouse,
Though life be wrenched away,
They cannot win the day.
The Kingdom's ours forever.

(LBW. P. 229).

Luther lived daily in the spiritual tension of the battle that he wrote about. Spiritual warfare was very real to him. In fact, it is said of him that he once threw an inkwell at the devil when he materialized in his room to tempt him.

While it is highly unlikely that this on-going battle between God and satan will ever become that "tangible" to most of us, it would do us well to recognize that *no one is exempt from satan's attacks.* No one.

Even those who are spiritually mature are targets for his "wiles", and quarry for his strategies, and perhaps more so, since they represent a greater threat to his malevolent purposes.

Satan's primary thrust in the world has not changed over the centuries. Since the Fall, he has been hard at work attempting to thwart God's plans in whatever diabolical ways he can.

The Apostle Peter, the most prominent of the twelve disciples, was often a target of satan's schemes, and had this warning for the New Testament Church:

> *"Be self-controlled and alert. Your enemy the devil prowls around like a roaring lion looking for someone to devour. Resist him, standing firm in the faith, because you know that your brothers throughout the world are*

undergoing the same kind of suffer-ings."

(I Peter 5:8-9).

Today, there are varied opinions about whether the devil exists at all. But to Jesus, and to those who, under the inspiration of the Holy Spirit, penned the Words of Scripture, there was no doubt that he was real.

* * * * * * * * *

The following scriptures are some of the refer-ences in which Jesus, Himself, referred to the devil:

"The weeds are the <u>sons of the evil one</u>, and the <u>enemy</u> who sows them is the devil."

(Matt. 13:39).

"Then He will say to those on His left, 'Depart from me,' you who are cursed, into the eternal fire prepared for the <u>devil</u> and his angels."

(Matt. 25:41).

"I saw <u>satan</u> fall like lightening from heaven."

(Luke 10:18a).

"Jesus said, 'Now is the time for judgment on this world; now the <u>prince of this world</u> will be driven out.'"
(John 12:31).

"When he comes, (the Holy Spirit) ... he will convict the world in regard to judgment ... because the <u>prince of this world</u> now stands condemned."
(John 16:11).

* * * * * * * * * *

In actuality, satan's most effective weapon today, may just be deceiving modern man into believing he doesn't exist at all.

* * * * * * * * * *

What better way to ensure that we will not stand against him and his sly enticements?

What better way to ensure that we will not take up our spiritual weapons (Eph. 6:11-18), and stop him in his tracks?

If you don't know you're in a battle, chances are, you're not going to arm yourselves and be ready to fight.

In this way, satan often gains the advantage.

* * * * * * * * * *

While many in the church are busy arguing and debating the validity of Scripture on this subject, the devil has gotten the "drop on us" – and is, in many arenas, moving in "for the kill".

> *Pretty good strategy, huh?*
> *Like taking candy from a baby...*

* * * * * * * * * *

Again, satan is a master strategist whose primary goal is to establish a rival rule to God's Kingdom.

* * * * * * * * * *

Whether we are aware of it or not, satan is not only in a life and death struggle with believers, but is also on a collision course with God, Himself. *He's mighty, but his days are numbered.* He was dealt a death blow from the cross, but he's not quite "down for the count" – yet!

* * * * * * * * * *

When I was a child, we lived in a rural area of Saginaw, Michigan. Having significant acreage, we were week-end farmers. At one point, we tried our hand at raising chickens. Now being quite young, I was fairly well sheltered as to where our Sunday chicken dinners really came from.

One Saturday afternoon, however, I got educated real quick!

I can remember, vividly, looking for my Dad, who had been seen earlier, heading toward the chicken coop.

As I rounded the corner of that building, I was just in time to see my Dad raise an axe, and bring it down with a "thud", on the neck of a chicken stretched across a makeshift butcher block.

What amazed me the most, was that for quite a while after the poor critter had been beheaded, his body continued to flop around. Somehow, his body hadn't quite gotten the message that he was dead!

His head lay motionless in the dirt, but he still expended quite a bit of energy jumping around, before he finally fell to the ground, and accepted his fate.

* * * * * * * * *

In a way, satan is in the same position. *From the cross, Jesus decimated his kingdom, cut off his dominion, and secured from him the keys of death and hell.*

He's lost the fight, but his pride will not allow him to accept his fate. He's still jumping around like a "chicken with it's head cut off".

But in due time, the Enforcer – Jesus

*Christ, the Victorious Lord of All –
will come and execute the warrant
against him, and he'll be relegated to
the Lake of Fire forever.*

* * * * * * * * * *

In the meantime, his ferocity and cunning grow
with each new day, for he knows his time grows
short.

He has an arsenal of sleezy counterfeits, seduc-
tive snares, wily temptations, and cunning decep-
tions – and a thousand variations of each besides –
all to use against God's people.

*Make no mistake about it – he's no
slouch! He is a formidable foe.*

* * * * * * * * * *

When satan was created by God, way back in
primordial times, he was not corrupt as he is today.
Quite the contrary, he was holy and perfect in all
his ways. There was not even a hint of sin or trea-
son or selfishness to be found in him.

*"You were blameless in your ways
from the day you were created, until
unrighteousness was found in you."*
(Ezek. 25:15 NASB).

Not only was he created holy, but he was created a cherubim – the highest of God's created order. Cherubim are superior in many ways to mortal man.

Further, he seems to have been a unique cherubim, because he is referred to as the "anointed cherub". So he was, actually, the highest and best of the cherubim.

One can surmise, that he was second in command in regards to the heavenly host, taking orders only from the Godhead.

> *"You had the seal of perfection, full of wisdom and perfect in beauty...*
> *Every precious stone was your covering."*
>
> (Ezek. 28:12,13).

* * * * * * * * * *

Scripture doesn't tell us when it was that satan (or Lucifer, as he was called then), was found to have unrighteousness in him – but it was sometime before Adam and Eve fell into sin in the Garden of Eden.

We know from Job 38, the whole company of angels witnessed and rejoiced at the creation:

> *"Where were you when I laid the foundation of the earth?*

When the morning stars (angels) sang
together, and all the sons of God
(angels) shouted for joy?"
(Job 38.4,7).

* * * * * * * * * *

Yet later, this adversary of God, set his snare for God's beloved, coming to them in the form of a serpent, and they succumbed to his cunning deceit.

The nature of satan's sin is clearly delineated in Scripture:

"Your heart became proud on account
of your beauty, and you corrupted your
wisdom because of your splendor."
(Ezek. 28:17 NIV).

In the fourteenth chapter of Isaiah, the prophet pens a discourse that has a dual reference. It refers to a future "King of Babylon", but at the same time, it gives a description of the historical fall of satan. It is commonly referred to as the five "I Wills":

"How you have fallen from heaven,
O morning star (Lucifer), son of the
dawn!
You have been cast down to the earth,
You who once laid low the nations!
You said in your heart,

> *"I will ascend to heaven;*
> *"I will raise my throne above*
> *the stars of God;*
> *"I will sit enthroned on the*
> *mount of assembly –*
> *on the utmost heights of the*
> *sacred mountain.*
> *"I will ascend above the tops of*
> *the clouds;*
> *"I will make myself like the*
> *Most High".*
> *But you are brought down to the grave,*
> *To the depths of the pit.*
> (Isa. 14:12-15 NIV).

These five statements summarize satan's sin. At some point, he became enamoured with his own beauty and capabilities, and rebelled against God.

* He wanted to usurp the Most High's position and authority.
* He wanted complete control over all other created beings – and he wanted to answer to no one.
* He wanted to sit in the place that was reserved for the Godhead alone, and to share equally in the glory that was given to God.
* He also wanted total rulership over the affairs of men.

In short, at some point, satan became dissatisfied with being only second in command. He wanted to be "like the Most High".

The irony is that because sin was found in him, he could never be like the Most High. At best, he could only have been a counterfeit deity – *as God has no sin, and is perfect in all His ways.*

I'm sure that for the devil, this adage rang true:

> *"The toughest instrument in the orchestra to play, is second fiddle".*
>
> (Anony.)

Not only did satan rebell against God, but he also corrupted one-third of the angelic host – and convinced them to attempt a "coup".

In the following description of that warfare, satan is depicted as a dragon:

> *"Then another sign appeared in heaven; an enormous red dragon with seven heads and ten horns and seven crowns on his heads. His tail swept a third of the stars out of the sky and flung them to the earth...*
>
> *"And there was war in heaven. Michael and the angels fought against the dragon and his angels, and they fought back.*

"But he was not strong enough and they lost their place in heaven. The great dragon was hurled down – that ancient serpent called the devil, or satan, who leads the whole world astray. He was hurled to the earth, and his angels with him."

(Rev. 3:4,7-9 NIV).

As a punishment for their attempted coup, and after a cataclysmic battle in heaven, with the Archangel Michael leading God's loyal angels, sentence was pronounced on satan and his fallen angels.

They were cast out of heaven in shame, and no longer allowed to abide there. They were also, ultimately, relegated to the Lake of Fire, forever.

* * * * * * * * * *

At present, satan operates in the "mid-heavenlies", and also on the earth, hence his two names, *"the Prince of the Power of the Air"*, and *"the Prince of This World"*.

"As for you, you were dead in your transgressions and sins, in which you used to live when you followed the ways of this world and of the <u>ruler of the kingdom of the air</u>, the spirit who is now

at work in those who are disobedient."
                                    (Eph. 2:2).

"Now is the time for judgment on this world; now the <u>prince of this world</u> will be driven out."
                                    (John 12:31).

* * * * * * * * * *

Many people think that satan hangs out primarily in hell – not so! He can get much more accomplished shuffling between the mid-heavenlies and the earth – after all, that's where the "catch" is!

* * * * * * * * * *

From his domain in the mid-heavenlies, satan wages war against the saints. He delays answers to prayers, and intercepts, as much as possible, God's angelic messengers, who continually travel between the Highest Heaven and the earth, in order to minister to believers and intervene in the affairs of men.

Read Daniel, Chapter 10.
Apparently, *upon permission from God, the devil is allowed limited visits to the Highest Heaven.* While there, he accuses God's people, just as he did Job, and, no doubt, must also answer to God regarding his activities and plans.

One should not assume, however, that satan has much freedom in heaven these days. He's only allowed to be there when it suits the Father's holy purposes.

He's nothing more than a pawn that God uses at His own discretion.

God keeps him on a short leash!

* * * * * * * * * *

Satan also roams around the earth, looking for weak-willed or unwary believers that he can deceive and tempt to evil, and looking for opportunities to oppose and pervert the Gospel and those who preach it.

Why should the devil spend his time in hell? The inhabitants there aren't going anywhere.

They are forever destined to suffer torment.

Satan may visit the "bowels of the earth" occasionally, but only to assert his devilish authority – or to conjur up some new and more gruesome torture that he can gleefully inflict on those who are bound there forever.

It's how he gets his kicks – that, and finding <u>new</u> prey to populate hell.

His time is short. He knows he must use it wisely ... there's no sleeping on the job for him!

* * * * * * * * * *

Double-Edged Temptations

"The Nature of Temptation"

The New Merriam-Webster Dictionary defines the word "tempt" in the following way:

1) to entice to do wrong by promise of pleasure or gain
2) to provoke
3) to risk the dangers of
4) to induce to do something; incite

Syn: inveigle, decoy, seduce, lure

Although the devil's schemes include much more than enticing temptations, for the purposes of this discussion, we will focus on that particular "wile". (A "wile" is "a trick or a stratagem – a sly deceit" of some sort).

Now satan, as a created being, is superior in many ways to humans, but God has sought to "level the playing field", by revealing in His Word the three primary devices of the enemy.

And remember, when it comes to spiritual warfare, knowledge is power. The more we know about the devil and his sly strategies, the more likelihood there is that we can recognize his ambushments before we become ensnared.

* * * * * * * * * *

I John 2:16, reads as follows (in the Amplified translation):

"For all that is in the world – the <u>lust of the flesh</u> (craving for sensual gratification), and the <u>lust of the eyes</u> (greedy longings of the mind), and the <u>pride of life</u> (assurance in one's own resources or in the stability of earthly things) – these things do not come from the Father, but are from the world itself."

* * * * * * * * * *

Satan's Basic Devices
are

1) <u>The Lust of the Flesh</u>
2) <u>The Lust of the Eyes</u>

3) <u>The Pride of Life</u>

Each of these is a mighty weapon in the enemy's arsenal – they're mighty because they have a long history of being effective in tempting believers to sin.

* * * * * * * * * *

Let's get specific by use of an example.

A sin which is on the increase in corporate America today, is theft. It goes by the name of "embezzelment", and is commonly referred to as a "white collar crime".

It can be defined as "stealing the company's money or assets".

Now, applying satan's three basic devices to this sin, let's see how the temptation might play out:

- "C'mon, take the money. You'll never get that raise anyway. The company is downsizing." (The Lust of the Flesh – instant gratification; Pride of Life).
- "You deserve this money, you've worked hard." (Pride of Life).
- "Just think of everything you could buy with that money ...". (The Lust of the Eyes).

Satan usually tempts us to quick actions, the easy way out, and "short cuts".

What he doesn't want us to know, is that when it comes to sin, the rewards are always short-lived, but the consequences are always long term and much more costly than imagined. He usually blinds the sinner to the full impact of the consequences that will come as a result of giving in to his temptation.

The devil is a sly and devious character, and we must guard ourselves from falling into his age-old traps.

* * * * * * * * * *

Satan has a whole series of traps laid for the unwary. He's not interested in getting the believer to sin only once, but he knows that with each trespass, it makes the next one all that much easier.

* * * * * * * * * *

One sin leads to another.

Stealing the company's resources, for instance, leads to falsifying the records, which leads to lying and more cover-ups.

He has a slippery slope – and a downward spiral – waiting just around the corner, for the one who, unwittingly, takes that first step into sin.

Such is the nature of temptation.

* * * * * * * * * *

But did you know that there are two sides to temptation?

It's like a double-edged sword, so I call them:

"Double-Edged Temptations"

On the one hand, in any temptation, there is the enticement to sin, but on the other hand there is also a testing that God allows because He intends to bring spiritual good out of the situation for us.

All temptation is double-edged.

God and satan are working in the same situation – one, for our good health and life; the other, for depravity and our death.

Temptation, then, is both an enticement to sin and a proving ground.

All temptation comes from satan. God tempts no one to sin, but God does use the opportunity to "test and try" us.

- *He wants us to see the "stuff" we're made of (He already knows).*
- *He wants to bless us when we have success-fully resisted evil.*
- *He wants to prepare us for what lies ahead. Trials such as this strengthen our faith and*

increase our dependence on Him.

Soldiers are not trained in the barricks, but on the obstacle course – and on the battlefield.

> *"But He knoweth the way that I take; when He hath tried me, I shall come forth as gold."*
> (Job 23:10 KJV).
> *"When tempted, no one should say 'God is tempting me'. For God cannot be tempted by evil nor does He tempt anyone; but each one is tempted when, by his own evil desire, he is dragged away and enticed (by satan). Then, after desire has conceived, it gives birth to sin; and sin, when it is full-grown, gives birth to death."*
> (James 1:13-15).

* * * * * * * * *

In spite of his power, satan is limited. He can only entice us to sin. He cannot force us to do that which is contrary to our will.

Jesus died that we would have a choice in every situation – and not be forced into the slavery of sin.

* * * * * * * * *

"The Nature of Christ's Temptation"

Jesus said that *"the servant is not greater than his master"*. In other words, He was declaring that many of the things He was to suffer, those who followed Him, would also suffer.

Temptation is one of those things.

Following Jesus' public baptism by John in the Jordan River, the Holy Spirit led Him *"into the wilderness to be tempted by the devil"*. (Matt.4:1).
Notice the phrase, "to be tempted by the devil". *Even though the Spirit led Jesus to the place of temptation, it was not God who did the tempting. It was the age-old enemy of God – satan.*

* * * * * * * * * *

Why, then, would the Spirit of God deliberately lead Jesus into battle with Satan?
Because, Temptation is Double-edged!

On the one hand, Jesus is led into a horrific battle with the evil tempter – a massive, well thought out attempt to entice Jesus to abandon the Father's plan for Him. But on the other hand, God uses this whole temptation scenario to test, try, and to begin to qualify Jesus to be the true and acceptable Sacrifice for our sins.

Unless He could not only recognize satan's fiendish wiles, but successfully stand against them – especially at a time of great physical testing and weakness, how could He hope to endure all that lay ahead?

> *If He stumbled in the desert,*
> *how could He handle the cross?*

In actuality, the truth is, that if Jesus were to have stumbled (into sin) in the wilderness, there could be no cross!

God's plan for the salvation of mankind would have had to be abandoned!

If Jesus were to succumb to any one of satan's enticements, at any point in His life on this earth, *He would have been rendered disqualified as our sacrifice for sins.*

He would no longer have been that sinless, unblemished Lamb, that the Law required as a substitute for our sins.

Can you see how critical this battle was?

God allowed this temptation experience in order to "test the metal" of His son.

Being now, "of human nature", He had to learn, just like you and I, how to gain mastery over the flesh, how to be obedient to the Spirit – and how to wage war against the attacker. <u>*And win*</u>*!*

* * * * * * * * *

He also had to endure temptation for our sakes. *The Spirit led Him into the wilderness in order to equip Him; not only for His earthly ministry, but to equip Him for His eternal ministry as well – that of being Chief Intercessor for God's people.*

* How could He effectively intercede for the saints if He had not personally experienced satan's temptations?

* How could He possibly encourage and help us unless He, Himself, had been there in the hard place, and come out victorious?

> *"For we do not have a High Priest who is unable to understand and sympa-thize and have a shared feeling with our weaknesses and infirmities and our liability to the assaults of temptation, but One who has been tempted in every respect as we are, yet without sinning."*
> (Heb. 4:15 AMP).

<u>God has His own holy purposes in whatever He allows to touch our lives</u>.

What the devil means for ill, God means for good.

* * * * * * * * *

This, dear readers, is the Double-Edgedness of temptation.

* * * * * * * * *

Now, as it says in the Word, Jesus had just been baptized by John, and it was His submission to baptism that ushered in His public ministry. Let's see why.

Jesus was fulfilling all righteousness – He was submitting to the law. You see, in sacred history, the High Priest always began his ministry with a special ceremony involving ritual cleansing. What it signified, was a formal "setting apart" of that individual "unto service".

(Exo. 29:4-7).

So, in essence, Jesus' submission to John and His submersion under the waters of the Jordan, was His unspoken and symbolic acceptance of the mantle that God desired to place upon Him – the Mantle of Messiahship – the Mantle of the Savior.

No wonder the Father was pleased!

* * * * * * * * *

It was directly on the heels of this Supernatural manifestation of divine unity, that satan launched his attack against Jesus.

"I need to put a stop to this charade now," the devil vowed to himself, "before any more damage is done."

Hence, the wilderness temptations.

* * * * * * * * * *

Jesus was probably many days into the wilderness, before He began to "come down" from the spiritual "high" associated with His baptism. The Father was pleased with Him, and publicly declared it to be so.

How it must have touched the heart of Jesus for His Father to have given such profound and unsolicited approval.

But now, here He was, many days away from that exhilarating experience, in a barren and rocky wasteland, with an empty stomach that was just beginning to "snarl".

He had successfully passed the tests of submission and humility – but what of the tests that lay ahead?

"Yea, all of you be subject one to another, and be clothed with humility; for God resisteth the proud, and giveth

grace to the humble.
(I Peter 5:5 KJV).

"Humble yourselves in the sight of the Lord, and He shall lift you up."
(James 4:10 KJV).

"Christ Jesus, who, being in very nature God, did not consider equality with God something to be grasped, but made Himself of no reputation, taking the very nature of a servant, being in the likeness of humans; and being found in appearance as a man, He humbled Himself and became obedient to death – even death on a cross."
(Phil. 2:6-8).

* * * * * * * * * *

To be sure, the devil didn't miss a move that Jesus made throughout that forty day ordeal. He watched silently and ominously – slinking around invisibly – but still there, nonetheless.

He wanted this victory so badly, that he could taste it. Ah, but the timing had to be just right.

It was still too soon to make his move.

Jesus wasn't weak enough yet.

Or hungry enough … *yet.*

"How dare He leave the throne room! How dare

He leave His divinity, and all that glory, behind! And show up here, in <u>my</u> domain, and as a mortal, no less!" the devil growled to himself.

"That's all right," he mused. "He'll be just as weak and susceptible to my temptations as all the rest ... after all, he <u>is</u> human now."

* * * * * * * * *

I rather think that Jesus had a lot of decisions to make regarding His ministry, don't you? Critical decisions. Life and death decisions. Strategy decisions.

He was about to "go public" with His ministry – a ministry so important that it would affect the lives and the eternal destinies of every person who would ever live.

For Him, personally, He knew nothing would ever be the same again.

He desperately needed the Father's wisdom, the Father's reassurance, the Father's plan – but mostly, He just needed the Father ...

* * * * * * * * *

So, for forty days and forty nights, He worshipped, communed, wept, fasted, and prayed – devoting Himself fully to the only One who could give Him the courage and the stamina to face all that lay ahead.

He knew that He had to be strong in every way –
physically, mentally, spiritually, and emotionally.

*So, He endured the solitude of the wilderness,
the burning, hot days and the frigid nights, the
snakes, the scorpions – and the hunger*, which, by
this point, was beginning to get harder and harder
to manage.

But He knew He had to gain a degree of mastery
over His body and His flesh that He had previously
not attained.

*The only food that He had to sustain Him
throughout this prolonged time of fasting, was the
Word of God*, and He meditated on that day and
night – and He soon discovered that it was enough.

No – it was <u>more</u> than enough. It was strength to
His bones and life to His soul!

And He gloried in the joy He found, as He kept
God's Sacred Laws ever before Him.

* * * * * * * * * *

When the full forty days had passed, and the
devil could take the suspense no longer, he was
ready to play his trump card:

> *"If you <u>are</u> the Son of God, command
> these stones to become bread."*
> (Matt. 4:3).

It is hard to say what rattled satan the most –

Jesus' ready response to him from the Word, or the conviction with which He spoke it:

> *"It is written: Man shall not live on bread alone, but on every word that comes from the mouth of God."*
> (Matt. 4:4).

With such an amazing aim and accuracy did Jesus wield the Sword of the Spirit, that the tempter had no apparent response, verbal or otherwise.

Score: Jesus 1, devil zip!

Next, satan changed topics, and tactics:
"The 'Lust of the Flesh' didn't work, so let's try the 'Lust of the Eyes'," he strategized, nervously. "After all, everybody enjoys being the center of attention …".

> *"If you are the Son of God," he said, "throw your self down. For it is written: He will command His angels concerning you, and they will lift you up in their hands, so that you will not strike your foot against a stone."*
> (Matt. 4:5,6).

Jesus answered him,

> *"It is also written: 'Do not put the*

Lord your God to the test'."

(Matt. 4:7).

Again, Jesus counters the second attack decisively with the Word, and the devil has no conceivable rebuttal.

Score: Jesus 2, devil 0

Are you surprised that the devil knows the Word? He does, but he only knows the "Letter of the Law". Therefore, he misapplied Psalm 91, even though he quoted it correctly.

God never intended that text to be used
as a rationale for tempting Him.

Jesus, on the other hand, knew both the "Letter of the Law" and the "Spirit of the Law", and could, therefore, counter the devil's ignorance with the Word "rightly given and rightly applied".

(Let's go back, now, to the desert).

By now, the devil is frantic, but trying everything in his power not to show it. He's running out of ideas, and his arsenal is almost depleted, but he still has one weapon left – the "Pride of Life".

"Aha!" He cries, with raised eyebrows. "I've got it! I'll offer Him a short cut. He can have all the kingdoms of the world, if He'll only bow down and worship <u>me</u> ... I'll get Him to transfer allegiance...".

"C'mon, Jesus. Everything that you see – all the kingdoms of the world can be yours, right here, right now, for the incredible, low price of only one tiny, little, worshipful bow. It's just you and me out here. Who else is gonna know?"

"I'm really thinking of you, now, Jesus – and here's the beauty of the plan, and the part that is sure to appeal to you:

"You don't <u>have</u> to go to the cross. With my plan, you can avoid all that pain and suffering and shame – and still have it all!"

"So, what do you say?" the devil ventured, with obvious pride in his plan.

> *"Away from me, satan!"* Jesus thundered with righteous indignation, *"For it is written: Worship the Lord your God, and serve Him only."*
> (Matt. 4:10).

Then, Scripture says, *"The devil left Him, and angels came and attended Him. (vv. 11).*

Final Score: Jesus 3, devil 0

* * * * * * * * * *

118

Jesus barely got the "Sword" back in it's sheath, before the devil was out of there.

(Now, not that I care, mind you, but, if you're the devil, and you've just been summarily defeated, I wonder where you go to hide until your wounds are healed?).

And just think! Jesus accomplished that victory after going forty days without food.

What A Savior!

* * * * * * * * *

A re-cap of the wilderness scenario:

Temptation	Type	Practical Application	Jesus' Weapon
1) To turn stones to bread	Lust of the Flesh (taste)	Use power for personal gain	The Word (Deut. 8:3)
2) To cast Himself down from the temple and test God	Lust of the Eyes (sight)	Dazzle multitudes with awe – use the spectacular instead of drawing people to God through faith	The Word (Deut. 6:16)
3) To worship the devil	Pride of Life (egoism)	Avoid the cross, transfer allegiance from God to the devil – abort God's salvation plan for mankind	The Word (Deut. 6:13)

As you can see, satan used all three of his basic stratagems against Jesus in this attack, but he was soundly defeated as *Jesus stood His ground and used the Word of God as a mighty weapon against him.*

In essence, Jesus used the only offensive weapon against satan and his attacks that is available to the believer. In Ephesians, it's referred to as the Sword of the Spirit.

Jesus used it with accuracy and precision, and also wielded it in faith.

It got the job done.

* * * * * * * * * *

"Finally, be strong in the Lord and in His mighty power. Put on the full armor of God so you can take your stand against the devil's schemes. For our struggle is not against flesh and blood, but against the rulers, against the authorities, the powers, of this dark world and against the spiritual forces of evil in the heavenly realms.

"Therefore, put on the full Armor of God so that when the day of evil comes, you may be able to stand your ground, and after you have done everything, to stand.

"Stand firm then, with the belt of truth buckled around your waist, with the breastplate of righteousness in place, and with your feet fitted with the readiness that comes from the Gospel of Peace.

"In addition to all of this, take up the shield of faith, with which you can extinguish all the flaming arrows of the evil one. Take the helmet of salvation and the sword of the spirit, which is the Word of God, and pray in the Spirit on all occasions with all kinds of prayers and requests.

"With this in mind, be alert and always keep on praying for all the saints."

(Eph. 6:10-18).

Satan never had a chance!

"Lessons From the Wilderness"

As we've said earlier, satan has been very successful in deceiving and corrupting mankind. He's been doing it for centuries. He's had plenty of time to study his prey. He knows how we think. He knows, most of the time, how we will react in various situations. Human nature hasn't really changed that much down through the ages. So, he has a lot of experience going for him, when he sets his traps for us.

But Jesus really gave us the _Keys to Victory_ through His own stunning triumph in the wilderness.

* * * * * * * * * *

How exactly did Jesus win that battle?

5 Keys to Victory Over Temptation

1) *Jesus was well-versed in Scripture, and spoke the Word accurately, forcefully, and in faith, against satan.*

2) *Jesus resisted temptation immediately.* He didn't dialogue with the devil about sin.

3) *Jesus was submitted ("dependent upon" and accountable) to the Father.* The wilderness only gave Him a greater opportunity to fellowship alone with God, apart from the hectic routine of life and the press of the crowd. *He was in constant fellowship with the Most High.*

   "Submit yourselves, then, to God. Resist (take the initiative) the devil, and he will flee from you."
                                    (James 4:7).

4) *Jesus was led by the Spirit.* He honored the presence of the Holy Spirit in His life by obeying His directives.

5) *Jesus prayed and fasted in order to gain mastery over His flesh.* As His spirit gained

more and more control over His carnal desires and physical appetites, all that Satan offered Him must have seemed unappealing and base.

If we will put into practice these _Keys to Victory_, we can experience just as much success over satan and his fiendish strategies as Jesus had.

* * * * * * * * * *

Another Famous Temptation

The Bible relates the story of another famous temptation – one that also had far-reaching and eternal implications for every person who would ever live.

It is the Temptation of Adam and Eve in the Garden of Eden.

The outcome of that satanic attack, however, was much different from the outcome that Jesus won in His wilderness experience.

Adam and Eve sinned. And because of their sin, the whole human race was plunged into death.

Jesus successfully resisted satan, remained sinless, and ultimately, became our Sin Substitute through His atoning death on the cross.

So, while death came to all men through the first Adam, life everlasting was won through the Second or Last Adam – Jesus.

> *"For since death came through a man, the resurrection of the dead also comes through a man. For as in Adam all die, so in Christ all will be made alive."*
>
> (I Corin. 15:21-22).

Why was one successful against the enemy of our souls and not the other?

Both had a human nature. When Jesus walked this earth, it was as a true man.

The result of one battle was death. The result of the other battle was life.

The stakes were equally high in both assaults – both were cosmic in scope and eternal in extent.

But the first Adam suffered a devastating defeat,

And the last Adam won an overpowering victory.

What made the difference?

* * * * * * * * *

Let's look again at the *Five Keys to Victory Over Temptation* that Jesus practiced in His glorious upset over satan, and see where Adam and Eve were, in relation to these prescriptions:

Key #1:

- *Jesus was well-versed and accurate with Scripture, and He spoke the Word to satan in faith.*

- When satan tempted Eve in the Garden, she omitted some of God's Word, then she added to it, and finally she lessened the power of God's Word in defining the consequences of the sin she was contemplating.

> *"Now the serpent was more subtle than any beast of the field which the Lord God had made. And he said unto the woman, Yea, hath God said 'Ye shall not eat of every tree of the garden'?"* (vv. 1).

> *"And the woman said unto the serpent, we may eat of the <u>fruit trees</u> of the garden."* (vv. 2).

> *"But of the fruit of the tree which is in the midst of the garden, God hath said, 'Ye shall not eat of it, <u>neither shall ye touch it, lest ye die</u>'."* (vv. 3).
>
> (Gen. 3:1-3 KJV).

Now, let's see what God actually said, and where the discrepancies lie:

> *"And the Lord God commanded the man, saying, 'You may freely eat of <u>every</u> tree of the garden, but of the Tree of the Knowledge of Good and Evil you shall not eat, for in the day that you eat of it <u>you shall surely die</u>'."*
> (Gen. 2:16,17).

In verse 2, Eve omitted the word, "every", when relating to satan God's goodness in allowing them to eat of every tree except the Tree of the Knowledge of Good and Evil.

Her focus was not on everything available for her to eat; it was already on the one tree that was "off-limits".

In verse 3, when she was answering the devil's "loaded question", she added the words "neither shall ye touch it". God never said that. Apparently at this point, Eve was already beginning to feel restricted by God's command, and so, here, she gave voice to that feeling.

Lastly, in verse 3, Eve changed a very significant phrase in God's command. She stated, "lest ye die", when God had actually said, "for in the day that you eat of it", (the fruit of the Tree of the Knowledge of Good and Evil), "you shall surely die."

She lessened the consequences of that disobedience.

* * * * * * * * *

Satan, whom we said earlier knows the Word, picked up immediately on her inaccurate and loose interpretation of God's Word, and he moved in for the kill, tempting her to eat. Then, he blatantly lied about the consequences of that sin.

He called into question God's motive in not allowing them to eat of that one tree. Satan planted the thought in Eve's mind that she was missing out on something wonderful.

The rest is history.

* * * * * * * * *

Now, in case you're wanting to place all the blame on Eve alone, it must be said that Adam didn't fare much better. He had the opportunity to say "no" to the invitation to join his wife in sharing the forbidden fruit, but he didn't.

Secondly, Scripture says, "The Lord God commanded the <u>man</u>". (Gen. 2:16a). As the spiritual head of that family, it was up to him to accurately and demonstrably communicate and teach God's ordinances to his wife.

Was there a communication problem between the first parents? Or was there a failure to place adequate importance on the specifics of God's Word from the very beginning?

Either way, there was enough vulnerability that it allowed satan a stealthy access to their collective will.

Key #2:

- *Jesus resisted temptation immediately. He did not dialogue with the devil about sin.*
- Eve joined in a discussion with the evil one regarding the sin that she was already entertaining. Instead of refusing the thoughts that satan planted in her mind regarding God and the fruit, she allowed them to "take root" mentally, and then empowered them by her words. She did not resist temptation immediately, as Jesus did. And Adam, perhaps by his silence, gave his approval to this conversation, and, ultimately, joined in eating the forbidden fruit.

Key #3:

- *Jesus was submitted ("dependent upon" and accountable) to the Father, and in constant fellowship with Him.*
- Scripture doesn't tell us how long Adam lived before God created Eve from his rib, but, suffice it to say, that he bore the greater responsibility of relationship with the Creator, both because of the

time factor, and his headship in the family. God structured order in the family by creating Adam first – so a greater obligation to walk in fellowship and submission to the Father rested with him.

The fact that Eve could begin to question God's motives is an indication that there was already a break in fellowship with God. And the fact that satan found her alone indicates that there may have been a break in fellowship with her husband. Had they stayed together, perhaps they could have gleaned satan's deception, and stood in unity against him until he was forced to flee.

Truly, once we leave the safety of fellowship with others and with God, we are an easy "mark" for the devil.

Instead, it was Adam and Eve who fled – from the presence of God because of their guilt, and, to the shelter of leafy trees to hide their nakedness and shame.

For the first time ever, SIN reined in the body, soul, and spirit, of a human being – and death entered the experience of man.

Key #4:

- *Jesus was led by the Spirit. He honored the presence of the Holy Spirit in His life by obeying His directives.*

- Who led Eve to the forbidden tree? It surely was not God.
- Why was she there? Had she been secretly savoring that fruit when satan found her there? It would seem so. By failing to avoid the "appearance of evil", she and Adam succumbed to the actual sin itself.

Key #5:

- *Jesus prayed and fasted in order to gain mastery over the flesh.*
- Since at this time in the Garden, there was no "sinful flesh" to gain mastery over, fasting would have been non-existent and irrelevant. But, with the opportunity and potential that Adam and Eve had for conversing with the Creator, either one, or both, would have found a listening ear and a compassionate Counselor, if they had only chosen to share with Him this visit from the serpent before they took the bait.

But sin is a slippery slope – and, obviously, once you start the downhill slide, it's impossible to "catch" yourself in time – especially if you've left God out of the picture altogether.

Again, if we will use our Lord as a model in dealing with the sly stratagems of the devil, we will have the same victory that He had.

*What the first Adam didn't know
And didn't do,
Jesus did!*

* * * * * * * * * *

And even though "In Adam we die,
in Christ Jesus we can be made alive."

Glory to His Name!

Dealing With Double-Edged Temptations

Principles to Remember

- *No one is exempt from satan's cunning attacks*, but we can have a plan in place for when those attacks come.
- *Satan does his best work when he can get us to believe that he does not exist.*
- *Satan is limited in what he can do.* He can only entice us to sin. He cannot force us. He was dealt a death blow from the cross. Jesus will execute that warrant when He returns as Victorious Lord of All.
- *Satan's end is the Lake of Fire*, and he knows it.
- *Satan has no authority over the believer* – and no power, either, as long as we are submitted to God, and resist him with the Word, and a godly lifestyle.
- *Satan operates both in the mid-heavenlies and on earth.*
- *Satan is just an instrument that God uses when it suits His holy purposes.*
- *Every temptation is double-edged.* There is both an <u>enticement</u> to sin and a <u>testing</u>.
- *God tempts no one, but He does use the situation to "test our metal".* He wants to bless us, teach

us, and prepare and equip us through the test.
- *Satan has three basic strategies in tempting us.*
  1) The Lust of the Flesh.
  2) The Lust of the Eyes.
  3) The Pride of Life.

(I John 2:16).

- *Jesus successfully overcame all three. If He overcame them, so can we.*
- *The rewards of sin are always short-lived, while the consequences are long term.*
- *The Holy Spirit led Jesus into the place of temptation in order to :*
  1) *Begin to qualify* Him as our Sin Substitute.
  2) *To equip Him* for His earthly ministry.
  3) *To equip H*im to be our Chief Intercessor.
  4) *To teach H*im how to gain the victory over temptation and the devil.
  5) *To show us* how we, too, can win over the attacks of the enemy.
- *The devil chooses the timing of his attacks carefully, so be alert.*
- *We have an arsenal of weapons to use against satan* – the most important is the Word of God wielded accurately and in faith. The rest are listed in Ephesians, Chapter 6.
- *Jesus gives us <u>Five Keys to Victory Over Temptation</u>.* Put them to work for you now, before the attack comes.
- *Where Adam and Eve failed and plunged*

mankind into sin and death, Jesus succeeded and won everlasting life for those who accept it.

- *Satan knows the Word.* He often misquotes and misapplies it.
- *Satan often tempts us to act quickly, selfishly, and promises short cuts.*
- *Satan is a master planner who has a whole network of snares laid out for the believer.*
- *No matter how devious satan is, he is no match for the Christ in us.*
- *Never fear satan, just resist him with the Word of God and he will flee.*
- *On the other side of the temptation successfully resisted*, is great reward.

The Weapon of the Word – To Help You Stand Against Temptations

(Speak these verses out loud twice a day.)

"But He knoweth the way that I taketh; when He hath tried me, I shall come forth as gold."
(Job 23:10 KJV).

"Submit yourselves to God, resist the devil, and he will flee from you."
(James 4:7).

"For we have not a high priest which cannot be touched with the feelings of our infirmities; but was in all points tempted like as we are, yet without sin."
(Heb. 4:15).

"For in that He Himself hath suffered being tempted, He is able to succor them that are tempted."
(Heb.2:18 KJV).

"There hath no temptation (test or trial) taken you but such as is common to man; but God is faithful,

who will not suffer you to be tempted above that ye
are able; but will with the temptation also make a
way to escape, that ye may be able to bear it."

(I Cor. 10:13).

"Blessed is the man that endureth temptation; for
when he's tried, he shall receive the crown of life,
which the Lord hath promised to them that love
Him."

(James 1:12 KJV).

"Put on the whole armor of God, that ye may be
able to stand against the wiles of the devil."

(Eph. 2:11).

"The Lord is far from the wicked; but He heareth
the prayer of the righteous."

(Prov. 15:29 KJV).

"Rejoicing in hope; patient in tribulation; continu-
ing instant in prayer."

(Rom. 12:12).

"...He preserveth the souls of His saints; He deliv-
ereth them out of the hand of the wicked."

Chapter Four

Struggling With Secret Shame
And Low Self Worth

When You Don't Like What You See In the Mirror

"The Problem Defined"

One of the most common and fundamental problems affecting mankind today, is low self worth. *The world is full of people who secretly struggle with the feeling that they just don't measure up.*

Surprisingly, a lot of Christians suffer from poor self images and live defeated lives because, at the very core of their beings, they are corrupted by negative thought patterns, and see themselves as losers.

If these feelings of inferiority go unchecked and unchallenged, the consequences can be dire – not only for those individuals, but also for their families, the church, and society as a whole.

For the Bible says:

> *"As a man thinketh in his heart, so is he."*
> (Prov. 23:7 KJV).

In other words, we tend to live up to the mental image, or self-portrait, that we have of ourselves.

What we see, feel, and think about ourselves is what plays out in our lives.

If we see ourselves as winners, we'll make winning decisions that bring satisfaction and contentment to our lives.

If we see ourselves as losers, we'll make losing decisions that bring frustration and inadequacy.

* * * * * * * * * *

The internal portrait, or mental picture, that we have of ourselves is critical in determining the quality of life we can have in this world.

> *In essence, what we tell ourselves about ourselves becomes a self-fulfilling prophecy.*

We will never rise above our attitudes concerning ourselves. As someone once put it, *"Our attitude determines our altitude."*

* * * * * * * * * *

> *Low self worth actually imprisons us and keeps us from exercising the freedom to succeed.*

It can paralyze us in one of two basic ways, by causing us to focus on "self-negativities", rather than on the potential that is ours in Christ.

When we suffer from deep-seated inferiority, generally, _we will either not step out to do the things that God would have us do,_ because of the fear that others will see what we are "really" like; _or we will become driven to excel, using those achievements in a self-promoting way to define our value._

There is not usually any middle ground for the soul trapped in the snare of secret shame.

Needless to say, if we see ourselves as deficient and useless, our agenda – which may be quite unrecognized and subconscious – becomes all important.

And God help the poor, hapless, individual who unwittingly gets in the way of our hidden quest for self-aggrandizement.

The quality of our relationships with others, then, becomes seriously strained.

* * * * * * * * * *

Did you ever try to establish a relationship with someone who did not like themselves? It's very difficult.

If we're constantly driven to protect ourselves from what we perceive to be the "prying eyes" of people who wander too close, it sends the message that we are "loners".

And expending all that energy toward self-protection and the maintaining of invisible barriers that keep people at arm's length, leaves us emotionally drained, with nothing left to give to others.

* * * * * * * * * *

In actuality, people who suffer from inferiority and inadequate self-concepts, are very self-centered.

Their value, to a large extent, is based on their own personal strengths and weaknesses. And, therefore, as we said earlier, they can become obsessive about excelling. They perceive failure as fatal – because performance is what their self-worth is based on, and it is that which justifies their existence.

They become cruel task-masters to themselves.

It's a sad and subtle form of "work's righteousness", which drives the afflicted one to more and more accomplishments – because the moment one is no longer able to adequately perform, one's justification for living is called into question.

Performance-oriented individuals usually have a strong shame base, which distorts and minimizes even the best of their accomplishments.

It is this shame base that constantly promotes the self-lie that "there is something wrong with you".

And no amount of lofty accomplishments can ever satisfy and fully counter the perception of "a defective self".

* * * * * * * * * *

Over the years, I have counseled with many, who would stare their rather remarkable accomplishments in the face and say, "They're all right, but it's too bad I'm such a failure at being a human being."

It was a nebulous, but nagging tape that would play over and over in their minds, making very short-lived the joy of any successful endeavor.

Such is the reality of a negative, shame-based orientation.

* * * * * * * * * *

For the person haunted with secret shame, life becomes a joyless journey, and an endless cycle of driven-ness, accomplishment, and despair.

Most who suffer from this malady, have become very adept at hiding these feelings of inadequacy and self-contempt, because the fear of rejection is too great to allow any degree of openness and vulnerability.

These secretly tormented individuals are already too self-rejected to risk what they perceive to be further pain.

And so the inner, self-depreciating tape continues to play unchallenged: "If I share with others what I <u>really</u> feel about my defective self, they will see what's wrong with me, too, and reject me."

For the self-contemptuous individual, then, no accomplishment, no matter how noteworthy, can fully satisfy that inner voice that goads one into continued despair: "You just don't measure up".

* * * * * * * * * *

Let's examine some of the factors that may cause us to feel second-rate, and inflict deep wounds in our sense of personal value:

• *Negative Childhood Experiences* –

Children who are raised in homes where disapproval, criticism, neglect and abuse exist, nearly always grow to have very inadequate self concepts.

Since we first learn about our own value based on how we are treated by the key people and care-givers in our young lives, the quality of our primary inter-personal relationships is central to how we see ourselves.

If we are treated with disdain, constantly

reminded that we are a disappointment to the family, rejected, or just made to feel "different" than the rest, not only will we internalize those negative judgments, but we will start to feel contempt for ourselves, and probably have difficulty "meshing" well in relationships later in life.

If we have difficulty in getting our basic needs met, our self worth will, invariably, be called into question.

• *Broken Dreams and Perceived Failures* –

In spite of the fact that disappointment is a part of every life, some find it more difficult than others, to move beyond these setbacks.

It depends, to a large degree, on how deeply one has been invested in those dreams and aspirations.

I have been in therapy with clients who were unable, for one reason or another, to fulfill a life-long dream, and that perceived failure rendered them unable to move forward in life, and it changed them forever.

For many, the pain of broken dreams can be just as real as the pain and sense of loss that accompanies the death of a loved one – and it's complicated by the fact that the resulting grief is harder to express.

When a loved one dies, there is usually a

funeral service of some sort, sympathy cards and flowers, hugs, and a bundt cake or two from the neighbors.

But when the bottom has fallen out of your long-planned career goals – or you come home from work one day and your husband of seventeen years is waiting for you with his bags packed – *what outlets exist to express that pain?*

People in our society – and certainly people within the church today – do not, for the most part, tend to gather around the suddenly unemployed or the newly divorced, with the same sympathetic support that they do the newly widowed. *But the pain is every bit as real – and, perhaps greater – because of the sense of failure that often accompanies the dissolution of that relationship, or the loss of that job.*

In the absence of effective and established outlets to express such pain, unexpressed grief turns to unresolved grief, which can, in its severest form, become self-destructive and can even compromise one's desire to live. The downward, emotional spiral from "rut to grave", can be subtle, swift, and deadly.

• *Unhealthy Comparisons* –

Children who are raised in homes where they are unfavorably compared with others, will grow to have self-defeating thought patterns regarding themselves.

If you constantly hear, "Why can't you be like "so-and-so", it is death to your sense of self worth, and it's not long before you're asking yourself the same question.

And usually, when we ask that question of ourselves, we will not bode well in that comparison, because we will always tend to compare the positive traits of others to our own negative traits. It's like comparing apples and oranges, but we don't see the difference.

The fact that we feel compelled to compare ourselves to others at all, rather than rejoicing in our God-given uniqueness, means we will usually come up "on the short end of the stick", so to speak.

The comparison game is always self-defeating.

• *Non-Christian Cultural Values* –

Every society has a list of standards that are considered desirable,and even necessaary, for success within that culture.

Although the standards vary widely from country to country, "westernized" cultures seem to promote the following:

- You must be young or youthful to have value.

- You must be thin to be attractive and desirable.
- You must dress for success, sporting "designer labels", if you want to "be somebody".
- You must have a certain skin color to be widely accepted.
- You must have connections to the wealthy and powerful if you want to succeed.

Skewed advertising campaigns blanket our society and reinforce these values, that can often leave people feeling like "misfits" or "defective", if they do not see themselves – or, if others do not see them – as conforming to these arbitrary standards.

Doors of education, employment, opportunity, and recreation can be opened or closed, based on how well it is perceived that an individual conforms to these unwritten social mores.

Growing up heavy in a thin world, for instance – or growing up poor in a world that exalts wealth and materialism – can promote unhealthy distortions in a person's self-esteem.

The result can be a slow, but steady decline in basic human dignity, and an ever-declining sense of the inalienable worth that God ascribes to every human being.

• *Satanic Interference* –

There is an age-old enemy of men's souls, that is hard at work today in the world, because he knows "his time is short".

He lies, deceives, twists, tempts, ensnares, and specializes in dream-stealing. He wants to render us ineffective and keep us from stepping out in faith toward our established destinies.

Scripture says that he is the "accuser of the brethren". (Rev. 12:10). *He accuses us before God, accuses us to others, and vice versa, but he also lies to us about ourselves.*

He will bring up our past mistakes, embellish our failures, and put every obstacle he can in our path, so as to prevent any forward movement on our part, toward our God-given destinies.

His goal is the destruction of God's people, and so he discourages, and seeks to undermine any healthy feelings of self that we may have.

But, Scripture says, that if we stay submitted to God, we can "resist him and he will flee".

(James 4:7).

The tricky part, however, is discerning his strategies. Because satan is able to put thoughts in our minds, many do not recognize the origin of these negative self-concepts. And, in not recognizing these "lying darts" of the enemy that foster self-doubt and condemnation, we do not, then, take authority over them.

What is not immediately recognized and resisted, remains and gets empowered; thus, a snare is set to defeat the believer in his own mind:

"You'll never do anything for God."
"You're not smart enough."
"You don't measure up."

These are the lies that keep us paralyzed – and hold us back from our established destinies.

And the villain behind these lying strategies goes unnoticed as being satan himself.

* * * * * * * * * *

Now the above list is by no means an exhaustive presentation of the factors that can propel us to low self worth, but they are some of the more widely recognized contributors.

* * * * * * * * * *

"The Power of Truth"

At the heart of every shame-based orientation and every problem of low self worth, is a lie.

It is the lie that "we don't measure up". It hints at some defectiveness that is so basic to our nature, that no matter how much we excel, the reality and power of that worthlessness will always override any good that we might accomplish.

It is the lie that tells us that we are second-rate, and therefore, are not deserving of success, happiness, satisfaction, and even God's grace.

Gone unchecked, it will keep us out of the boardroom, the breakroom, and the throneroom.

In other words, it will inhibit our success and leadership abilities, it will keep us from enjoying healthy relationships with co-workers and friends, and it will have tragic implications in terms of our relationship with our Heavenly Father.

* * * * * * * * * *

Now, the only thing that is stronger and more enduring than a lie, is the Truth.

Ultimately, it is God who establishes, or "sets

up" Truth.

You and I may have a variety of opinions on various subjects, society may seek to preserve the ever-changing standards that become the accepted norm of the day, but it is God, and God alone, who establishes Objective Truth.

He, by virtue of His Sovereignty, His Omniscience, and His Creative Genius, is the only One in a position to do so.

* * * * * * * * * *

This is what God says about us:

> *"See what (an incredible) quality of love the Father has given (shown, bestowed on) us, that we should (be permitted to) be named and called and counted the children of God! And so we are!"*
>
> (I John 3:1 AMPL).

> *"For we are His workmanship, created in Christ*
> *Jesus for good works, which God prepared beforehand that we should walk in them."*
>
> (Eph. 2:10).

> *"For ye are the temple of the living*

God; as God hath said, I will dwell in them, and walk in them; and I will be their God, and they shall be my people."

(II Cor. 6:16 KJV).

Greater is He that is in you, than he that is in the world."(I John 4:4). "For ye are bought with a price ..."

(I Cor. 6:19a).

In these selected verses, and many, many others in Scripture, God pours out His feelings for each of us. The Bible is His love letter to us.

God states catagorically that He created us, He loves us, and, as believers, His Holy Spirit dwells in each of us. In other words, "The Greater One" is on the inside of each and every believer.

* * * * * * * * *

How is it, then, that we can have such low regard for one whom the Lord cherishes so much?

Friend, what is it that determines the value of anything in our world?

Isn't it the price that we are willing to pay to purchase that item?

Well, God loved us so much that He paid the ultimate price to make us His own forever. He sacrificed His only begotten Son, as a Sin Sacrifice for us, in order that we, through Him, might be saved.

That's quite a price to pay.

And that makes each soul of infinite value to the Creator.

> *"For God so loved the world,*
> *that He gave His only Son,*
> *that whoever believeth in Him,*
> *should not perish, but*
> *have eternal life".*
>
> (John 3:16).

"YOU ARE GOD'S MASTERPIECE!"

Scientists tell us that no two people are exactly alike, even identical twins. No two sets of fingerprints are the same, no two voiceprints are the same, no set of DNA – the basic "stuff" of heredity – identically matches the DNA of another human soul, living or dead.

* * * * * * * * * *

You are unique.

You are not a mistake, nor an afterthought.

You are no less than what a Holy, Creator God intended you to be.

* * * * * * * * * *

You are God's Masterpiece – quite literally, a little "piece of the Master" - with the spirit and life of the Creator inside you.

* * * * * * * * * *

Let's look at what God has invested in you:

Long before the world ever came to be, way back in eternity past, the Triune Godhead came together in perfect unity, and thought of you.

As God poured over all the limitless possibilities, He settled on a specific design for your body that appealed to Him, and He carefully selected the winsome pecularities in your personality that pleased Him.

He created the entire blueprint for your life, carefully weaving the rich tapestry in the way that would bring Him the most glory – and, as He stood back to admire His handiwork – He couldn't help but fall in love with His creation.

Then, with absolute confidence and trust in you, He placed upon you a special "mantle", a "calling", if you will – a destiny, that only you could fulfill, in order that your life would have meaning and purpose, and that the world might be a little better place because you lived.

He further placed, within you, special and unique talents, interests, and abilities, that would ensure your success, as you walked out that established destiny ...

And He loved you!

Then, in Holy Jealousy, He did one thing more. He carved out a special place in your heart just for Him.

Without so much as a second thought, He staked out a little piece of geography just for Himself – there, in the tender recesses of the deepest part of you.

He wanted to ensure that you would never feel complete – and never be fully whole – without Him.

That's how much He longed for a relationship with you.

Then, He stood back, took one last look at the object of His love, and sealed the finished product until the day of your birth.

He chose two parental "co-creators" to assist in your future arrival. And His heart burned with Holy Desire at the very thought of you.

And, lastly, as He looked forward, from eternity into time, and focused on your entrance into the world, *He gave final approval for the Creation of*

You – and He smiled, and rejoiced, at the thought of your birth.

* * * * * * * * * *

With the very Creator God loving you this much, how can you feel so badly about yourself? Stop playing God, and accept the limitless value that He has already ascribed to your life. He not only lovingly formed you – He paid the ultimate price to "buy you back" to Himself from sin, death, the grave, and satan.

The devil is at the heart of every negative self-thought you have. If he can get you to believe a lie, and speak it over yourself, he can bring those lies to pass in your life.

But that's not surprising, is it? This is what Jesus had to say about satan:

> *"He was a murderer from the begin-ning, not holding to the truth, for there is no truth in him. When he lies, he speaks his native language, for He is a liar, and the father of lies. Yet because I tell you the truth, you do not believe me."*
>
> (John 8:44-45).

Satan is cunning enough to change the methods he uses from time to time, to keep you feeling inadequate. He can not only plant negative, self-condemning thoughts in <u>your</u> mind, but he will also use others, as it suits him, as "tools" to destroy your confidence.

* * * * * * * * * *

Any statement of reality which does not line up with the Word of God (our standard for objective truth), is a lie. That lie must be cast down and it's power over the hearer broken.

* * * * * * * * * *

If you grew up in a troubled home, for instance, and you were taunted with the words, "You will never amount to anything", we would immediately reject that statement as a lie from the enemy, spoken by some troubled human vessel duped into use by the devil.

Why is that statement a lie?

Because God said in Jeremiah 29:11;

"For I know the plans that I have for you, declares the Lord; plans to pros-per you and not to harm you; plans to give you hope and a future."

Further, as believers, we already <u>are</u> "something". We are the righteousness of God in Christ Jesus. (II Cor. 5:21).

* * * * * * * * * *

So, then, if a statement disguising itself as truth, doesn't line up with our standard of truth (God's Holy Word), then we simply stand against the lie, and refuse it, in the Name of Jesus, using a declaration similar to this one:

> *"I refuse that lie, satan, in the Name of Jesus, for it is written, 'We are the righteousness of God in Christ Jesus'."*

We address our declaration to satan, because Scripture says that:

> *"We wrestle not against flesh and blood, but against the rulers, against the authorities, against the powers of this dark world and against the spiritual forces of evil in the heavenly realms."*
>
> (Eph. 6:12).

* * * * * * * * * *

Can you see why satan would want to launch a

massive attack against children?

If he can get them to hear lies at an early enough age, they will believe those lies and spend the rest of their lives trying to sort it all out. They'll be terrified to do anything, and paralyzed by the propaganda they have internalized.

And, unless there is an intervention of the truth to counter those lies, those children will make self-defeating decisions that ensure failure throughout their lives.

Many homes today are like war zones, instead of being the "mini-arks" that God intended them to be, where His precious ones can be safely sheltered from the storms of life.

It's a sad commentary, when one discovers that whatever is "out there in the world" is preferable to what goes on inside the confines of their own family.

Parents, needless to say, ought to be the biggest-supporters – not the severest critics – of their children.

* * * * * * * * * *

Accordingly, words are vehicles of power. They have no neutrality. They are either vehicles of positive power or energy, or vehicles of negative power.

Once they are spoken, they are launched out into the spirit realm. They are like arrows. After they are released, like arrows from the bow, they cannot be brought back. They are eternal.

> *Remember, we are made in the likeness and image of the Creator – and God spoke everything into being with words.*

Scripture says that "the worlds were framed with the Word (of God)". (Heb. 11:3). Accordingly, our words have more power than you think. Words are actually seeds that produce after their own kind.

"There's a creative power behind our words", says Charles Capps, author of "The Tongue – A Creative Force".

"The power of life and death rests with the tongue", according to the Bible. (Prov. 18:21).

It is very possible to kill with words. Some of us on a bad day, can "take out" five or six people before 9:00 a.m.! But the Bible says, "Do not kill". It also says that we will be held accountable for every word which passes over our lips.

Satan wants to feed us a steady diet of lies – because once we start to believe them, and speak them, they become self-fulfilling prophecies in our lives. He wants to thwart the plans of God, especially in young lives.

* * * * * * * * * *

If words bring fear, torment, self-doubt and despair, they are from the devil, no matter who speaks them!.

God's words bring faith, joy, hope, and peace.

* * * * * * * * * *

Again, at the heart of every problem of low self worth, is the lying work of the devil.

Begin to speak out what God says about you. His words bring life and health.

* * * * * * * * * *

The good news is that we can change how we feel about ourselves. If we will get into agreement with God and His Word, and begin to speak that Word over us and meditate on it, we will see our low self worth begin to elevate.

* * * * * * * * * *

Overcoming Shame and Low Self Worth Principles to Remember

- *God defines truth and ascribes value.* We are of infinite value to Him.

- *God wants us to have a healthy self concept* that is in line with His Word.

- *You are a special and wonderful Creation of God.*

- Change your verbage about yourself – and *refuse to empower satan's lies in your life.*

- Our words are either vehicles of negative or positive power. *Speak only positively about yourself and others.*

- *Resist the devil when he plants a negative thought in your mind.*

- *Begin to confess that you are a winner in Christ Jesus.*

- *Begin to speak the Scriptures over your life.*

- *Stop comparing yourself with others.*

- Refuse to accept the devil's strategy of reminding you of *past failures and sins. They are "covered under the blood of Jesus".* If God has forgiven and forgotten them, shouldn't you?

- *Choose to stay away from negative people,* especially those who bring you down and make you feel defective, by their words or actions.

- *Spend regular time with God in prayer.* He loves you, thinks highly of you, and has the power to set you free from self-contempt. He can give you new thoughts about yourself.

The Weapon of the Word –
Helpful Scriptures to Meditate On and Confess
As You Move Toward A Healthy Self Image

- *"I can do all things through Christ who strengthens me."*
  (Phil. 4:13).

- *"But you are a chosen generation, a royal priesthood, a holy nation, His own special people, that you may proclaim the praises of Him who called you out of darkness into His marvelous light."*
  (I Peter 2:9).

- *"You did not choose Me, but I chose you and appointed you that you should go and bear fruit, and that your fruit should remain, that whatever you ask the Father In My Name He may give you."*
  (John 15:16).

- *"You are my servant, says the Lord. I have chosen you and have not rejected you. So do not fear, for I am with you; do not be dismayed, for I am your God. I will strengthen you and help you; I will uphold you with my righteous right hand."*
  (Isa. 41:9b-10).

- *"Fear not, for I have redeemed you; I have summoned you by name; you are mine ... You are precious and honored in my sight ... and I love you ..."*

  (Isa. 43:1b, 4).

- *"Forget the former things; do not dwell on the past. See, I am doing a new thing! Now it springs up; do you not perceive it?"*

  (Isa. 43:18).

- *"I, even I, am he who blots out your transgressions, for my own sake, and remembers your sins no more."*

  (Isa. 43:25).

- *"Can a mother forget the baby at her breast and have no compassion on the child she has borne? Though she may forget, I will not forget you! See, I have engraved you on the palms of my hands; your walls are ever before me."*

  (Isa. 49:15-16).

- *"Do not fear the reproach of men, or be terrified by their insults. For the moth will eat them up like a garment, the worm will devour them like wool. But my righteousness will last forever, my salvation through all generations."*

  (Isa. 51:7b-8).

- *"I, even I, am he who comforts you. Who are you that you fear mortal man, the sons of men, who are but* grass; that you forget the Lord your Maker, who stretched out the heavens and laid the foundations of the earth; that you live in constant terror every day because of the wrath of the oppressor, who is bent on destruction."
(Isa. 52:12-13).

- *"For as a man thinketh in his heart, so is he."*
(Prov. 23:7).

- *"For you created my inmost being; you knit me together in my mother's womb. I praise you because I am fearfully and wonderfully made; your works are wonderful."*
(Ps. 139:13-14).

- *"But God shows His great love for us, that while we were yet sinners, Christ died for us."*
(Rom. 5:8).

- *"No weapon formed against you shall prosper, and every tongue which rises against you in judgment you shall condemn."*
(Isa. 54.17).

- *"God has not given us a spirit of fear, but of power, love, and a sound mind."*
(II Tim. 1:7).

- *"Finally, brethren, whatever things are true, whatever things are noble, whatever things are just, whatever things are pure, whatever things are lovely, whatever things are of good report, if there is any virtue and if there is anything praiseworthy – meditate on these things."*

(Phil. 4:8).

Conclusion

While satan is a formidable foe, we can resist him successfully using the strategies presented in this manual.

The Word of God, rightly spoken and rightly applied, and wielded like a sword in faith, will quench "all the fiery darts of the devil".

With the return of our Lord closer than ever before, we can expect that satan's attacks will increase, and his strategies will become more insidious.

We must be alert, and ever-growing in holiness, in faith, and in God's Word.

Against such, he has no power.

God Bless You.

Prayer For Salvation

Heavenly Father, I come to you now in the Name of Jesus. I admit that I am a sinner and I confess Jesus as my personal Lord and Savior. I believe that He died on the cross for me and I believe that His shed blood is now washing me clean. Help me Lord to live for you. I give you my life and ask you to fill me with your Holy Spirit.

Thank you, Father. In Jesus' Name I pray, Amen.

* * * * * * * * *

If you prayed this prayer from your heart and meant it, you are now reborn! You are a Christian — a child of our Heavenly Father. You are saved and have a place with God for all eternity. Angels rejoiced when you gave your heart to the Lord, and your name was written in the Lamb's Book of Life.

Now, let your lifestyle and your actions confirm what you have just done. Read the Bible daily, attend a Bible believing church regularly — and pray. Talk to God about everything. He eagerly awaits.

Congratulations! And welcome to the Kingdom of God!

About the Author

Phyllis Rawlins has been teaching the Word of God since she was sixteen years old. She has been in full-time ministry for over twenty five years.

She earned a Bachelor's Degree from Western Michigan University in Kalamazoo, Michigan, and a Master of Divinity Degree from Trinity Seminary in Columbus, Ohio.

She has done post graduate studies at North Dakota State University, and in Atlanta, Georgia, where she presently resides.

She has served congregations in Michigan, Ohio, and North Dakota, and has served, most recently, as Director of Chaplaincy Services for a hospice agency in the state of Georgia.

She is also a licensed family therapist.

She travels throughout the world, preaching, teaching, and ministering powerfully under the anointing of the Holy Spirit, and has a strong burden to teach believers how to overcome adversity and all the attacks of the enemy.

Printed in the United States
1145600002B/259-459

9 781591 605461